A King Production presents…

A Novel

JOY DEJA KING

Cover concept by Joy Deja King
Cover Model: Joy Deja King

Library of Congress Cataloging-in-Publication Data;
King, Deja Joy
Stackin' Paper Part 4: a novel/by Joy Deja King

For complete Library of Congress Copyright info visit;
www.joydejaking.com Twitter: @joydejaking

A King Production
P.O. Box 912, Collierville, TN 38027

A King Production and the above portrayal logo are trademarks of A King Production LLC

This Book is Dedicated To My:

Family, Readers, and Supporters.
I LOVE you guys so much. Please believe that!!

—Joy Deja King

"Killas On Front Line When You're War Ready. Chopper Shoot A Thousand Rounds When You're War Ready. Just Another Homicide Cause We War Ready..."

War Ready

A KING PRODUCTION

Stackin' PAPER IV
War Ready

A Novel

JOY DEJA KING

Chapter One

Idols Become Rivals

The clouds were like great wings of gold, yellow, and rose color, with a smaller sprinkle in one spot, like a shower of glowing stones from a volcano. The mixture of fierceness and gloom in the sunset, call the mind of the coarseness of the man contemplating his next move.

"Mr. Douglass, your guest is here," Fatima said, walking the man out onto the terrace. "Can I bring you anything?"

"No, I'm fine and no interruptions," Arnez stated, putting his hand up to dismiss Fatima, his caretaker, away. "Caleb, have a seat," Arnez said after she was gone. "Thanks for coming by."

"Did I have a choice?" Caleb frowned up his face. "Two goons pulled up on me, damn near yanking me off the block and nah that's okay, I'd rather stand," he popped, folding his arms.

Arnez chuckled, finding what Caleb said humorous. "Your tough guy act is amusing. Now sit yo' ass down before I let you see what them goons that picked you up, is really capable of," Arnez warned.

Caleb squinted his eyes. He didn't like Arnez playing him like a chump but he also didn't want a confrontation with those goons, especially since they confiscated his gun. Caleb reluctantly sat down in the chair directly across from Arnez.

"Cooperating with me, is gonna make things go a lot smoother for you. Otherwise, it can get ugly real quick."

"Yo, what tha fuck do you want wit' me?" Caleb huffed, leaning back in the chair shaking his head. He couldn't figure out why this man, who he'd never met in his life, had basically forced him to come to his crib so they could talk.

"I see you're impatient, so let me get right to it," Arnez remarked arrogantly. "You know a man named Genesis Taylor?" Arnez already knew the answer but wanted to keep the wheels spinning in Caleb's head.

"You talkin' 'bout the drug kingpin Genesis Taylor?" Caleb questioned with confusion.

"Is there another Genesis Taylor?"

Caleb paused for a second as if considering the question. "Nah, I mean of course I've heard of Genesis. He's every dope boy's idol including mine, in these Philly streets. Every hustler moving weight wanna make it to his level. Why you askin' me about him?"

"Because you work for him."

"I don't work for Genesis. I've neva met that man a day in my life."

"The last part might be true but you do work for him."

Caleb licked his lips, folded his arms, and continued to frown up his face. "If you say so," he shrugged.

"Khyree gets all his product from Genesis and runs the major locations for him in Philly. You work for Khyree, so that means you work for Genesis."

"You know an awful lot 'bout what tha fuck

I do but I don't know shit 'bout you. What's the point to all this bullshit?"

"The point is, very soon you gon' be running those major locations for Genesis," Arnez nodded.

Caleb let out a soft chuckle. "Man, you got jokes."

"I don't joke about business. I'm dead ass serious."

"A'ight, let me amuse you for a sec. I'm damn near at the bottom of the totem pole in that organization. How the fuck am I gon' rise up to replace Khyree?"

"You leave that to me. Just know you'll be the last nigga standing, so you'll take the reign by default."

Caleb cut his eye at Arnez. He was still holding his arms but was now leaning back in his chair. He was balancing the back legs of the chair with the heel of his Nikes. None of this shit felt right to him and he wanted to understand what he was missing.

"Why me? I'ma seventeen-year-old block worker. I ain't got nothing for you."

"That's where you wrong. The blocks you work make the most money. You young but you got hustle and you hungry. That's why I chose you."

"Chose me to what?"

"To work for me. After I make you the point person to Genesis, you will then infiltrate his organization and give me everything I need to destroy him."

"Nigga, you fuckin' crazy!" Caleb jumped up and spit. "I'm outta here!"

"Sit down!" Arnez demanded. "Don't make me ask twice." Caleb still didn't budge. The speed picked up in his walk to get to the double doors.

Initially, Arnez figured he would be able to lure a young buck like Caleb into his lethal plan by simply enticing him with being the head nigga in charge. But that wasn't working, so now Arnez had to pull out the big guns. Ammunition he'd wanted to use at a later time but that time was now.

"How's your brother doing? I know it must be hard for him, especially hard for your mother and his daughter."

Caleb stopped mid step. "What you know about my brother?"

"I know he's in jail facing a lengthy prison sentence on an attempted murder charge. He got a court appointed attorney handling his case, no bail money. Khyree ain't offered to give yo' brother a dime. You makin' all that money, runnin' them blocks for him but he can't even throw you a bone to help out yo' brother. Don't you want your brother to come home?"

"Of course, I do. That's why I've been puttin' in all that work on the blocks. Tryna get my paper up, so I can get him some proper representation."

"How's that workin' out for you?" Arnez cracked in a cynical tone.

Caleb was pressing down his mouth and his jaw was flinching. He was angry but this time his rage wasn't towards Arnez. It was thinking about how Khyree did know the predicament his brother was in but didn't give a fuck. He had gone to his boss, asking if he could front him some money and let him work it off. Instead of Khyree lending a hand to his best worker, he told him he had his own problems to deal with and brushed him off.

"Can you really get my brother a good lawyer?"

"I'll do better than that. I'll get him out on bail and if you do as I say, I'll make those attempted murder charges disappear," Arnez promised.

"Now you have my attention." Caleb sat back down and listened intently to every word Arnez had to say. The devil had finally spoken the magic words and Arnez smiled with delight.

Chapter Two

I Need Closure

"You are still the most beautiful woman in the world," Genesis said, waking up while holding Talisa in his arms.

"You've said that every morning since I came back home and I'm not tired of hearing it yet. It sounds like the very first time, whenever those words come out your mouth."

"Because it is like the first time. Every day I wake up, I fall right back in love you all over again." Genesis gently kissed the top of her left shoulder. Time had passed but Talisa still seemed extremely fragile to him. Each touch was so tender and when they made love it was as if time had stood still.

"Ahhh," Talisa purred in his ear as Genesis entered inside her wetness. This had become their daily and nightly ritual. The sounds each made while lovemaking had become their favorite background music. The softness of Talisa's skin and the hardness of Genesis's dick was the perfect combination between their bodies to get lost within each other.

"I want to stay inside of you forever," Genesis stared in Talisa's eyes and said as they continued making passionate love, before falling back asleep in each other's arm.

"Time to wake up, beautiful." When Talisa opened her eyes, Genesis was standing up holding a hand sculpted, bronzed mirrored inlay serving tray with wooden rims.

"What's all this?" she smiled.

"Instead of going out, I thought I'd make

you breakfast in bed." Genesis sat the tray down and Talisa immediately began admiring the mouthwatering presentation.

"I completely forgot how great you can cook. This isn't your typical oatmeal and toast. More like a five-star gourmet meal," she remarked, looking at the turkey bacon and leek quiche, skillet buttermilk biscuits, challah bread French toast, roasted rosemary potatoes, and pancakes with maple-syrup pears and spiced ricotta. "I seriously doubt I can eat all of this, although I want to."

"Don't worry, I'll help you." Genesis got back in the bed next to Talisa.

"This food is delicious," Talisa gushed, before taking a sip of the mango mimosa.

"Glad you like it," Genesis said kissing her on the cheek. He doted on Talisa like they were teenage lovers. He couldn't help himself. It wasn't intentional. Genesis was in a rush to make up for all of their lost time together but in his heart, he knew time couldn't be replaced. "I was hoping to stay in bed with you all day but unfortunately I really need to tend to some business with Amir," he explained.

"You don't have to explain." Talisa turned to Genesis taking his hand. "You haven't left my side since I've been back. It's okay for you to work. I'll be fine."

"I'm sorry...."

"Don't apologize." Talisa cut Genesis off and said, "You have to stop feeling guilty for what Arnez did to me. It wasn't your fault. And please don't stop living your life because I'm back home."

"You are my life."

"You're my life too." Talisa stroked the side of Genesis's face. "But you also have to live your life and I need to start doing the same too."

"What does that mean? Do you have plans to go out today without me?" Talisa could detect the uneasiness in Genesis's voice.

"I was thinking about doing a little shopping, going to get my hair done," she said, tugging on her long braided ponytail.

"What's wrong with your hair? I think you look beautiful."

"Nothing's wrong, I haven't had a haircut in so many years. I'm ready for a change. Is that okay?"

"Of course." Genesis was quick to reassure her. "I didn't mean to sound overbearing. I can free up my schedule tomorrow and we can make a day of it together."

"Genesis, I'll be fine. You can't hold my hand

forever."

"Why not?" he laughed. "I know I can't hold your hand forever but work with me. I never believed I would hold or see you again. Now that I have you back, I refuse to ever let you go again. Call me overprotective," he admitted. "Of course, I'll have the driver take you wherever you need to go, in addition to security detail to escort you at all times. That's not negotiable."

"I see you're still the same stubborn, bossy man I fell in love with," Talisa smiled.

"I call it protecting the most precious thing in my life, which is you." He kissed Talisa on the tip of her nose. "I need to go take a shower and get ready or I'll never leave this bed," Genesis said, standing up.

"After I finish eating the rest of this delicious food, I'll be doing the same. But before you go take a shower I need for you to do something for me."

"Of course, what you need, baby?"

"I want you to tell Skylar I want to see her."

"Excuse me?" Genesis sat back down, not expecting that to be Talisa's request.

"You heard me. Soon she'll be the mother of your child which means they'll both be a part of our lives. I want her to know that I'm okay with that."

"Are you?"

"I wouldn't have said it if I wasn't."

"I see you're still the same sweet yet straightforward woman I fell in love with," Genesis smiled.

"Does that mean you'll do what I asked?"

"How can I tell my beautiful wife 'no'. Not only will I ask but I'll make it happen."

"Thank you."

Talisa did want to reassure Skylar that she would love the child she shared with Genesis like it was her own, but it wasn't the only reason Talisa felt the two women needed to speak. She hadn't forgotten Skylar left her to spend the rest of her life and to eventually die on the island she escaped from. In order for Talisa to get closure, Skylar had some explaining to do.

Genesis spent his entire day in one meeting after another but his conversation with Talisa, earlier that morning, remained in the forefront of his mind.

"James, take me to Skylar's place," Genesis instructed his driver staring out the backseat window. Throughout the duration of the car ride, until he reached her front door, he went over in his head what he would say to Skylar. But, when she opened the door, Genesis was so shocked with the immense size of Skylar's stomach, he basically forgot what he planned to say.

"This is a pleasant surprise," Skylar said with a smile after letting Genesis in.

"Wow, the baby..."

"I know," Skylar softly giggled. "I feel like the size of my stomach doubled overnight."

"I'm glad it's just not me. I know I haven't seen you in a few weeks but I wasn't expecting this. But you are pregnant and stomachs do get bigger. That means the baby inside of you is growing. I remember when Talisa was pregnant with Amir and..." Genesis's voice trailed off as he stopped himself.

Although it felt natural for Genesis to talk about Talisa's pregnancy, he knew under the circumstances, it had to be difficult for Skylar to hear it. "So how are you feeling?" he asked, trying to change the topic.

"I'm good. I'm ready for the baby to come. I'm excited to see her face," Skylar beamed.

"Me too. Did you receive all the baby furniture I got for her?"

"Yes, I did. Thank you. It was beautiful. I was

going to call you but I figured it might not be a good idea. Do you want to see the room? I got it fully decorated."

"I would like that." Genesis followed Skylar down the hall to the baby's nursery.

"I wanted it to be an oasis of peace and beauty." Skylar smiled when they entered the room.

The décor of the nursery was exquisite. The Victorian English chandelier, a perfectly proportioned design of mixed rustic iron and crystal glass that was precision cut and polished to give optimal sparkle, caught Genesis's attention first. His eyes then shifted to the heirloom white mirrored end panel crib, adorned with graceful, interlocking fretwork, which imparted an understated elegance. It was a striking combination of function and glamour. The little duchess upholstered cot, handcrafted with French silk, brushed chrome, and handmade quilting, then the blush and ivory color scheme gave the nursery a flawless finishing touch.

"I can tell you put a lot of thought into decorating her room. It's truly beautiful, Skylar."

"I think so too. I had imagined us doing everything together for the baby but I've accepted that for the most part I'll be doing it alone." Her voice sounded full of regret.

"That's not true. I will always take care of you and the baby."

"Taking care of a baby requires more than money, Genesis. When I found out I was pregnant, I expected us to be a family."

"We are family."

"Oh, please!" Skylar snapped, turning away from Genesis.

"Just hear me out."

"I'm sure whatever you have to say, I don't want to hear it." Skylar put her hand up and stormed off.

"This is important and the reason I came over to see you today. I really need to discuss something with you." Genesis wanted to calm the situation as he could see Skylar was becoming agitated.

Skylar stopped in the middle of the hallway and looked back at Genesis who was standing in the doorway of the nursery. "And here I thought you came over because you were concerned about me and the baby I'm carrying," she scoffed sarcastically.

"Skylar, I'm not trying to upset you, especially with you being so far along in your pregnancy. But Talisa wanted me to ask you if she could come over and speak with you."

"Speak with me about what? Not telling her the truth about you and leaving her on the island? Gosh Genesis, I don't want to rehash that with Talisa right now."

"I get that, but eventually the two of you are going to have to sit down and talk. Talisa is my wife and you're going to be the mother of my child. The three of us will have to get along and that means being open to communication," Genesis explained.

"I get that. But right now, all I want to focus on is giving birth to a healthy baby girl. My baby can come any day now and I don't want to be stressed thinking about my conversation with your wife."

"Okay, I'll let her know, but think about what I said too. Also, this is *our* baby." Genesis stressed the word our. "I will be in our daughter's life full time."

"How does your wife feel about that?"

"Talisa is an amazing woman and any child of mine she will love like it's her own."

"I see. Well, I'm glad you have it all figured out, but umm, you can see yourself out. I need to go lie down."

"Are you okay?"

"I'll be fine. I'm just feeling a little lightheaded," Skylar said before feeling a sharp pain and her legs buckle.

"Skylar, come sit down," Genesis said holding her up.

"Oh gosh!" They both looked down. "I think my water just broke," a stunned Skylar said to Genesis. Then the contractions kicked in and she howled out in pain. "The baby's coming!"

"Now? You think the baby is coming now?!"

"Yes! Call my doctor," Skylar moaned. Tell him I'm going into labor and you're about to bring me in," Skylar mumbled as her eyes kept opening and closing.

"Skylar...Skylar... are you okay?" Genesis was trying to get her to open her eyes, but she seemed to be out of it. Genesis was afraid for Skylar's life and the life of his unborn child.

Instead of calling Skylar's doctor, Genesis dialed 911. "My ex-girlfriend's waters broke, she went into labor and then she passed out. Please tell me what I need to do. I don't want her to lose our baby."

Genesis held on to Skylar, praying she would open her eyes and be able to deliver their baby girl.

Chapter Three

Family Ties

"Is it me, or did Genesis seem a bit preoccupied during our meeting?" Lorenzo questioned.

"Nope, that's just you," Nico popped back as he read a text he just received.

"Actually, you're right, Lorenzo," Amir stated. "He told me earlier that he wasn't staying for our last meeting because he needed to go speak with Skylar."

Nico glanced up from his phone when he

heard what Amir stated. "There's not a problem with the baby, is there?"

"I know she's due soon but my mother wants to meet with her before the baby comes," Amir revealed.

"I'm guessing that's what Genesis went to speak with Skylar about?" Lorenzo remarked. Amir nodded his head yes. "I see why your father was preoccupied. He has a wife and an expecting baby mother to deal with. I don't envy that."

That comment made Nico think back to when he was still in love with Precious but found out Lisa was pregnant. He always wondered if he had handled the situation differently, would it had stopped Lisa from lying to him by saying she had an abortion and leaving town. If so, he could've helped raise Angel, instead of being reunited with her once she was a grown woman. That scenario weighed heavy on Nico's heart.

"Hopefully Genesis gets all that shit worked out. I know he loves Talisa more than anything but he has an innocent child coming into this world that's gonna need him," Nico said, still reflecting on all his lost time with Angel.

"You know my father is gonna make sure that child doesn't want for nothing," Amir scoffed.

"Being a father takes way more than money,

it requires your time and dedication. Money is the easy part when you got an endless amount of it," Nico shot back.

"Whatever you say, Nico." Amir's attitude made it clear he wasn't too jubilant on welcoming the soon to be newest member of the Taylor family.

"Amir, I know you're grown in the legal sense of the word but you ain't *grown* like me," Nico stressed. "God willing, when you do become my age, you'll understand why it's so important for your father to be more than an ATM machine to your little sister. And yes, that is your sister, whether you like it or not."

"Nico is right, Amir," Lorenzo chimed in. "You've mentioned to me your concerns about Skylar and the baby and the affect it will have on your family but the baby is your family too. You're going to be a big brother and you'll have to protect your sister. I know you're a good man, Amir, so I trust you'll do the right thing," he added.

"Because you agreed with me, don't mean I like you now, 'cause I don't," Nico had to throw that part in." Lorenzo simply shook his head, not paying Nico any attention, and let him continue his rant.

"But umm, you do have to step up and be a

big brother. I keep stressing that shit to Aaliyah. The age gap is a lot wider between you and the new baby but just like you're going to be a big brother, Aaliyah is a big sister to Angel. That means you have to be a leader and act like you got good sense even if you don't," Nico huffed.

"I understand what both of you are saying and you're absolutely right," Amir said politely, wanting both of them to shut the hell up. He wouldn't dare let those words come out his mouth though, so instead he pretended to agree.

"That's my man!" Lorenzo stood up from his chair and patted Amir on the back. "I knew you would step up and do the right thing."

Nico sat with one eye up watching Amir smile and Lorenzo looking at him proudly. But Nico wasn't convinced by Amir's words of acceptance. Aaliyah was his daughter and he knew that both she and Amir were used to getting their way, by any means necessary.

"Sir, an emergency medical squad is on the way. Please go unlock the front door as you may not be in a position to do so when they arrive," the dispatcher instructed him. Genesis rushed to unlock the door and then ran back to Skylar who was waking back up.

"Where am I?" Skylar mumbled before immediately screaming out in pain as her contractions were coming fast and strong.

"Skylar, it's me, Genesis. You passed out. I think you're about to have our baby. I have a dispatcher on the phone now who is going to guide me until help arrives," he said calmly.

"Sir, go grab some towels, sheets, or blankets. Put one underneath your girlfriend..." Genesis was about to correct the dispatcher but at the moment, delivering a healthy baby was more important.

"Okay, I'm getting the stuff now. Skylar, I'll be right back," Genesis told her.

"Hurry! I think the baby is coming any minute. I feel this overwhelming urge to push!" Skylar cried, getting scared.

The dispatcher heard what Skylar said and instructed Genesis to try and put it off through panting, using breathing techniques, or lying Skylar on her side, but none of that shit was helping to stop that urge for Skylar to push. Genesis came back with towels, blankets, and sheets. He gently moved Skylar and placed a blanket underneath her.

"Ms., those methods you had Skylar do aren't working. The baby is coming," Genesis informed the dispatcher.

"Make sure she is propped up. You don't want the baby to fall and suffer a serious injury," she warned.

"Don't worry. I'm not going to let anything happen to my daughter. What do I need to do next?" Genesis asked.

"Take off her pants and underwear. Try to stay calm. Babies that arrive quickly usually deliver with ease but guide the baby out as gently as possible," she emphasized.

A loud scream from Skylar caught Genesis off guard. When he looked down, after removing her underwear, he could see the baby's head coming out. His heart was racing as Skylar's screams became louder and the dispatcher now sounded like she was speaking a foreign language to him.

Genesis, calm the fuck down. You're about to bring your daughter into this world so get yo' mind fuckin' right, he thought to himself, taking a deep breath.

"Gently guide the baby out," he heard the dispatcher say.

"I'm doing so but the umbilical cord is around her neck," he said trying not to panic.

"Try to ease it over the baby's head slowly or loosen it enough to form a loop so the rest of her body can slip through," she directed.

"Okay, I'm doing that now," Genesis said as his breathing was becoming more intense.

"When she's fully out, don't, I repeat don't, pull the cord, don't try to tie off or cut the cord. Leave it attached to your baby until the emergency medical crew arrives. Are you there, sir?"

"Yes, I'm here. I'm holding my daughter." Genesis was all choked up but managed to speak. Hearing the cries coming from the baby girl he just delivered had him feeling emotional.

"I understand, but you're not done yet. You must deliver the placenta which should come shortly. Leave the placenta attached to the cord too. Medical personnel will take care of it. But you can go ahead and dry your daughter off.

Genesis reached for one of the other blankets he had gotten and tenderly dried off his daughter. He was awestricken. He heard the dispatcher talking but he was stuck on staring at his baby girl, completely mesmerized at this tiny life he was holding in his hands.

"Sir!" the dispatcher yelled out after not getting a response from Genesis the first two times.

"My fault...what did you say?" Genesis finally

questioned, snapping out his trance.

"I need you to place your daughter on her mother's stomach, skin to skin so she can warm her with her body heat. After you do that, cover them up with a dry blanket."

Once Genesis finished doing what the dispatcher instructed, he watched as Skylar held their daughter and saw the love in her eyes.

"She's so beautiful," Skylar wept. "Thank you for delivering our baby girl. She's perfect."

"Yes, she is," Genesis smiled. "I don't know if you've chosen a name but I was thinking we could name her Genevieve after my sister."

"Your sister Nichelle?" Skylar asked.

"Yes. When she was born my mother named her Genevieve but when they left North Carolina and changed their identities, she became Nichelle. But the name Genevieve has always remained close to my heart and I would love for our daughter to have that name, but only if it's okay with you."

Skylar rested her eyes on their child before glancing back up at Genesis. "Genevieve, it is."

Genesis bent down on the floor where Skylar was sitting, holding their baby. At that moment, there was no other place he wanted to be, than with Skylar and Genevieve.

Chapter Four

Heavy Heart

After leaving the Chanel flagship store on East 57th Street, Talisa felt she had done more than enough shopping and was ready to do something a little more adventurous.

"You're right on time," the stylist said cheerfully when Talisa sat down in the chair.

"You sound surprised."

"Let's just say my clientele isn't the most punctual," she laughed.

"I'll admit, I'm pretty excited. I was actually early but I waited in the car," Talisa admitted.

"Glad you're excited. So, what are you having done today...wash, deep condition, a trim?" the stylist questioned as she unraveled Talisa's bun.

"I want my hair like this." Talisa took out a picture she tore out of a hair magazine and handed it to the hairdresser.

"You can't be serious!" she turned to Talisa in shock after eyeing the picture. "Girl, women be paying big bucks for bundles so they can have hair like yours and you want me to cut it off?!"

"It's just hair. It'll grow back. I'm in need of a change," Talisa decided.

"Are you sure you want something so dramatic? Your hair is simply gorgeous."

"I'm positive. Just leave enough where I can pull it back when I want to. So instead of it being right underneath my ears, cut it to the middle of my neck," Talisa suggested.

"Are you sure that will be enough hair for you to pull back?"

"Positive. Not long enough for a bun but enough to tie an elastic band around it. So, get to cutting!" Talisa beamed, adamant about her decision to go short for the summer. "I've had long hair my entire life. I'm ready to become a new woman."

Precious was on her way to look for something to wear to Aaliyah's upcoming wedding when she noticed a missed call from Skylar. "How did I miss that," Precious said out loud, about to hit her back when Skylar's name popped back up on her screen. "Hey! I was just about to call you back. Is everything good?"

"Everything is great. I'm at the hospital with my daughter." Precious could practically see Skylar smiling through the phone.

"You had the baby! OMG congratulations. Have you told Genesis yet?"

"I didn't have to. He delivered her."

"Genesis delivered the baby! Girl, say no more. Save that story until I see you in person. I'm gonna want to know every detail. I'm assuming you and the baby are doing wonderful?"

"Yes! Why don't you come see for yourself," Skylar told Precious.

"Say no more, I'm on the way. Text me the hospital info. Can't wait to see my Goddaughter! Be there shortly."

Precious hung up, ecstatic about seeing Skylar and the baby. With Aaliyah about to be a married woman, and Xavier off at college, Precious was starting to have baby fever. She had zero interest in becoming pregnant and bringing another child into this world but that didn't stop her from wanting to gush over one. Skylar's new bundle of joy was the perfect alternative.

It was Wednesday evening and Caleb did what he considered to be his only duty, checking in on his mother. He hadn't lived at home since he jumped off the porch at the tender age of thirteen. Like so many young boys growing up in the streets of Philly, Caleb was trying to survive. Surviving meant doing what you had to do to get by and for Caleb that was sticking up dope boys until he started selling drugs.

"Hey Ma," Caleb said kissing his mother on the cheek. "How you doin'?"

"Good, now that my baby here. Have a seat. I made your favorite meal," she smiled, disappearing into the kitchen. She came back a few minutes later with a hot plate of food.

"I got something for you." He put a few hundred dollars in her hand.

"Thank you, baby. You always look after yo'

mama," she gushed, kissing him on the cheek. "I always look forward to your visits, now if only we can get your brother home."

"I'm workin' on that, Ma. If all goes well, I'll make it happen."

Caleb reflected back on the conversation he had with Arnez a week ago. He hated to work for him because he knew the dude was a snake but he tried his way and shit wasn't proceeding as planned. Having a selfish boss like Khyree was the culprit. No matter how much grind Caleb put in, Khyee continued to take the majority of the cut, only dishing out crumbs to his workers, even his most proficient one like Caleb.

That's why Caleb promised himself, if he ever made it to the upper echelon in this drug game, he'd make sure to take care of his people. They would all eat good. There was never a guarantee of loyalty, especially when it came to street hustling but he figured the odds would be better in his favor if he treated his crew right. What he detested the most about working for Arnez though, was having to help him takedown Genesis. Although he didn't know him personally, Caleb had only heard great things about the man. Genesis was one of the very few men left in the game that had managed to reach a level of greatness where he almost seemed untouchable.

"I'm praying you can, Caleb. Your niece was over here earlier today."

"How's Amelia doing? I know she gettin' big," he grinned.

"Yes, she is. She such a pretty little girl. It breaks my heart when she looks at me with those big wide eyes and ask when her daddy coming home. She misses him so much and so do I." Her eyes watered up.

"Ma, please don't cry." Caleb pleaded. That was the reason he didn't stop by and see his mother more often. Ever since his brother Prevan got locked up, she would break down crying whenever he would visit. Then he'd feel like a failure for letting his mother down. The guilt would eat Caleb up.

"I'm sorry, son, but you the only person I can share how bad I'm feeling with. I try to be strong with everybody else but yo' mama hurtin' inside."

"I know. Did Celinda bring Amelia over or her sister?"

"Celinda came." Caleb's mother smacked her lips. "That girl ain't got no shame. It's her damn fault yo' brother in this mess. Let her tell it, she the victim though. I knew from the first time your brother brought her home, she was nothing but trouble," she said shaking her head.

"Yeah, I ain't feeling homegirl neither," Caleb agreed.

"Then she be speaking all that Spanish to Amelia and I don't understand nothing they be saying. Once my grandbaby let it slip that her mother had called me a nosey witch." Her face frowned up.

"Don't get worked up. Just try and keep the peace, so she'll keep letting you spend time wit' Amelia. Knowing his daughter's good, is what keeps Prevan's spirit up while he in jail."

"I know," his mother said putting her head down. "Trust me, if it wasn't for Amelia, I would've beat Celinda's ass a long time ago. Enough about her. All it's doing is gettin' me upset. How are things going with you?" she asked lovingly. "Have you found yourself a girlfriend yet?"

"Nah. I'm just out here grindin'. Ain't got time for no female drama," Caleb stated.

"You doing right, boy," she nodded. "You see what happened to yo' brother. Wait for the right girl to come along. Preferably one that ain't out here runnin' these streets."

Caleb didn't respond to what his mother said but he agreed with her. If and when he found himself a lady, Caleb wanted her to be a good girl.

Not cut from the same cloth as him. Most importantly she had to be loyal because disloyalty would get you killed.

Chapter Five

Word Of Advice

"Good afternoon! I hope my handsome husband is having a wonderful day." Astrid beamed, kissing Delondo on the lips. "I was thinking we could go out for dinner tonight. Just the two of us," she said massaging his shoulders while he sat behind his desk.

"Not tonight babe. I have to handle something." Delondo let out a heavy sigh.

"Is everything okay? You seemed stressed. I

can feel some tension in your shoulders."

"After Theron got killed, I thought things would start to get back to normal. Having a snitch in my crew and not knowing who it was had me under pressure," Delondo shared.

"But like you said, Theron is dead so that pressure should be too...right?"

"Yeah but now it's something else." Delondo's body slightly slumped forward wanting to release the unwanted tension.

"Baby, talk to me. What is it now?" Astrid questioned, pretending to be the devoted wife.

"There's this nigga, Khyree. He handles the majority of product Genesis moves in Philly. But I believe he's been moving in on my territory."

"Why do you say that?"

"Because I'm startin' to lose money in a few areas which means my business is going someplace else. There's no other crew in Philly that can supply that quantity to the streets besides Khyree."

"So what are you going to do?"

"First, I gotta make sure it's him. Maybe some new crew done rolled up in Philly although I highly doubt it. Once I confirm it's him, then I'ma step to dude."

"Do you think Genesis is aware of what

Khyree is doing?" Astrid asked.

"I doubt it. He moves so much product on the East Coast he ain't got time to micromanage Khyree. The only way he would step in, is if it was brought to his attention."

"Maybe you need to bring it to Genesis's attention. He might be able to resolve the situation before things get out of hand. It's just a suggestion," Astrid added giving Delondo another kiss.

"I appreciate you listening to me and for the suggestion," he smiled, kissing his wife's hand.

"I'm always here for you. Now I'm going to leave you to handle your business. Hopefully we can have our romantic dinner later this week. Call me if you need me." Astrid blew her husband a kiss before closing the door to his office.

Delondo sat back in his chair, staring up at the coffered ceiling made of carved stone, contemplating his next move. He then weighed in on the suggestion his wife made and decided it was worth taking into consideration. But instead of calling Genesis, Delondo decided to reach out to someone else.

When Talisa woke up she was startled Genesis

wasn't lying beside her. It was the first time that happened since she'd come back home. She then thought back to last night before she fell asleep waiting up for him. He did come home because she remembered feeling the softness of his lips on her neck while dozing off. But Talisa wanted to see his face and hear his voice. She got out of bed, thinking maybe he was making her breakfast or in his office wanting to get to work early. Talisa searched and called out his name but there was no Genesis in sight.

"Where are you?" Talisa questioned out loud reaching for the phone.

"Baby, hi," Genesis answered.

"I woke up and you weren't here."

"Talisa, I'm sorry."

"Did something happen...is everything okay?"

"Skylar had the baby yesterday. I came to the hospital to see Genevieve."

"You named her Genevieve after your sister."

"You remembered that," Genesis said.

"Of course, I remember. I remember every-thing you've ever said to me," Talisa stated in a melancholy tone.

"You know how much I love you, right?"

"I do but it doesn't even matter because

I love you enough for the both of us. Go spend time with your daughter. I'll be here when you get home."

Talisa hung up the phone and sat down on the couch. She was overcome with sadness. No matter how much Genesis loved her, Skylar was able to do something with him that Talisa never had a chance to...raise a child together. That fact broke her heart. He was at the hospital celebrating the birth of his daughter with another woman and there was nothing she could do about it. Right when she was about to breakdown and cry, she heard the front door opening.

"Who's there!" she called out.

"Hi, Ma, it's me Amir."

Talisa quickly wiped away the few tears that managed to escape her eyes and tried her best to erase any indication of sadness from her face.

"Amir, come give me a hug. I feel like I never see you enough. I can never get over how much you look like your father."

"Ma, you always tell me that," Amir grinned hugging his mother. "You cut your hair. I like it. What did dad say?"

"Nothing yet."

Amir raised his eyebrow. "What do you mean. I'm sure he's seen it and the cut is pretty noticeable."

Talisa turned away from her son before responding. "I was about to make something to eat. Are you hungry?" she asked heading towards the kitchen.

"No, I'm good. I already ate. Where's dad?" he questioned following his mother to the kitchen.

"I guess he hasn't had a chance to tell you."

"Tell me what?"

"Skylar had her baby. They named her Genevieve. I'm sure it was your father's idea. He always loved that name. He used to say if we ever had a daughter we would name her that."

And there it was. The last sentence triggered the tears. Once they started flowing, Talisa couldn't stop herself.

"Oh, Ma, I'm so sorry." Amir held his mother tightly.

"I feel so embarrassed. I didn't want to cry like this in front of you," she sobbed.

"You have nothing to be embarrassed about! I hate this is happening to you but you gotta know dad loves you. He loves you so much." Amir rubbed his mother's back, trying to ease her pain.

"I know he does and although he won't admit it, I know he loves Skylar too."

"No! No, he doesn't! He loves you and only you."

"Amir, it's okay. I know your father doesn't love Skylar the way he loves me but he does love her and now that they share a child together, the love will only deepen."

"What are you saying, do you think he's gonna leave you for her?"

"No. Your father and I are soulmates. He'll never leave me and I'll never leave him but things are going to be different. Genesis is a strong believer in family. Skylar and Genevieve are our family and they will be treated as such. Your father will demand it. That's the type of man he is and one of the reasons I love and respect him so much."

"But what about you and your feelings?"

"I'll be okay. For the last couple of months, I've been preparing myself for this day. I knew the baby was coming but I won't lie, it's hard. It's only going to get harder before it gets any easier," Talisa admitted.

"Don't worry, I'll be here for you. We'll get through this as a family," Amir promised.

"Back already!" Skylar beamed when Precious walked in.

"I couldn't stay away. My goddaughter is so freakin' cute. I had to come see her again. Where is she?"

"You're going to have to wait a minute. The nurse just came and got her. They had to run a few tests before we go home tomorrow."

"No problem," Precious said sitting down. "My day is open. How are you feeling? You look great for a woman that just gave birth yesterday."

"I feel incredible and Genesis has been amazing. Do you know he was here first thing this morning," Skylar said unable to contain the excitement in her voice. "He just left a few minutes before you came. I'm surprised you didn't run into him. He said he was coming back later on."

"Wow! That is a tad surprising. I mean, there's no doubt in my mind he's going to take his fatherly duties seriously but I figured it would lean more on the financial side."

"I thought the same thing too. But he's made it clear, he wants to be present in our daughter's life."

"That's wonderful. That beautiful little girl deserves to have a great father figure and it doesn't get much better than Genesis. But don't read too much into that, Skylar," Precious warned.

"What do you mean?"

"Genesis is very committed to being a father to Genevieve but he is in love with Talisa. His life is with her."

"Things can change."

"Listen, you know I was team Skylar and Genesis but that was before I saw them together."

"You saw Genesis and Talisa together? You didn't tell me," Skylar said becoming defensive.

"Because you were pregnant and I didn't want to upset you. I've been around them a few times and what they share is magical. I'm just keepin' it real. You my girl and I love you. I'll never feed you some bullshit. Talisa loves that man and Genesis loves her just as much. She is not gonna let a baby he made when he believed she was dead break her family up."

"I'm not worried about Talisa."

"Well you should be. I know her type. She comes across sweet and fragile and I'm sure she is. From what I've been told, she grew up rich and privileged. I'm not talking that street money or entertainment industry money, I'm talking that sheltered from the boogeyman type money. I doubt she's ever been in a fistfight her entire life but for Genesis, Talisa would kill for," Precious stated matter of factly.

"So, would I." Those words tumbled out of Skylar's mouth by accident but she meant every word.

Precious leaned forward, glancing down at her fresh French pedicure for a few seconds. She then played with the diamond stud in her right ear and started tapping her heel.

"Child, I'm 'bout to talk to you like you were my daughter. Cut that shit out! Genesis is taken. He is a married man. You do know him and Talisa remarried. It was a very small ceremony but it wasn't about that for them. He wanted to make sure that legally she was his wife. You have to respect that, Skylar. I know you feel you've been dealt a bad hand. You fell in love with a man you believed to be available. No one would've ever thought his wife would come back from the dead. Now you have this man's child and you're thinking there's still a chance you can get the happily ever after ending. I'm here to tell you, it ain't gonna happen."

"We both know things can change."

"True but not with them. It's like if some chick tried to come in and take Supreme away from me. I would dead that shit before it even had a chance to pop off. It's not gonna happen...

ever! I guarantee you, Talisa feels the exact same way about Genesis. So, enjoy your beautiful baby girl. Feel blessed you have a baby daddy who is going to make sure you and your child wants for nothing. Leave at that before you end up only having visitation rights to a child you carried for all those months and pushed out yo' coochie," Precious scoffed.

"You really think Genesis would fight me for custody of our daughter?" Skylar's eyes widened in suspicion.

"Right now, I would say hell no. He's not that type of man. But everyone has their limits. If you try to use Genevieve to break up his marriage, I'm not sure what Genesis might do. My advice to you is don't do anything that might cause you to find out."

Chapter Six

Devotion

"Sorry, I'm late." Genesis announced when he entered the boardroom where Nico, Lorenzo, and Amir were already seated.

"No apology needed, more like congratulations." Lorenzo walked over and gave Genesis a hug.

"Thank you, but how did you find out?"

"That would be me," Amir raised his hand up and said. "I saw my mother earlier today. She told me," Amir stated dryly.

"How's she doing...what's the little one's name?" Nico questioned.

"Her name is Genevieve and she's perfect. I'm actually the one who brought my baby girl into the world," Genesis boasted.

"You brought her into the world...you saying you delivered her?" Amir asked with disdain.

"Yep!" Genesis nodded proudly.

"Go 'head man!" Lorenzo grinned as Nico jumped up and shook Genesis's hand.

"You did that!" Nico smiled

"It was crazy. I was at her place and we were talking. Then Skylar's waters broke and things spiraled down from there. I managed to keep my cool and delivered a beautiful, healthy daughter. Skylar was remarkable throughout the entire ordeal. She's going to be a great mother to Genevieve."

While Nico and Lorenzo continued to relish in Genesis's story, Amir sat stone-faced thinking of the pain his mother was in.

"Lorenzo, didn't you say we needed to discuss some very important business?" Amir interrupted the trio and said.

"Yeah...yeah...yeah. I got a call from Delondo yesterday," Lorenzo informed them.

"What did Delondo want?" Genesis asked as the men took their seats.

"He believes Khyree is intruding on some of his territories. Before things go left, he wanted you to come down and meet with them," Lorenzo said.

"Why don't you and Amir go in my place," Genesis suggested.

"Why can't you go?" Amir wanted to know.

"Because I want to be here with my daughter."

"She's just a baby. She won't remember if you were with her or not," Amir popped.

"But I'll know," Genesis popped back. "The same way I was with you from the day you were born, I will be with Genevieve. Do you have a problem with that?"

"Nah, I ain't got no problem," Amir lied but the glare in his eyes didn't.

"Good, then you and Lorenzo can go to Philly today and get this situation dealt with. We don't need any problems. There's more than enough money to be made in the streets of Philly where everybody can eat good."

"Enough said. Amir and I will head to Philly," Lorenzo confirmed.

"We've got that out the way, what's next on the agenda?" Genesis questioned before Nico spoke up with a pending problem needing to be dealt with.

Although Amir was physically in the room and seemed to be listening to what was being said, his mind was somewhere else. He was seething at the notion his father was celebrating the birth of his daughter. He wanted no parts of the new baby but deep down Amir knew that was wrong. Genevieve was innocent in this fiasco, and in a way so was Skylar. It wasn't like she was a mistress, spreading her legs open for a married man and then got pregnant. Those facts didn't matter to Amir. To him, Skylar was a problem and now that she had her baby she'd become an even bigger problem. Unfortunately for Amir, he had no clue how to fix it.

"Where are you rushing off to?" Chanel wondered as she started getting undress to take a shower.

"Going to see Genesis. His daughter was born yesterday. I have to go pick up a gift I got for the baby before I stop by," T-Roc explained.

"How nice. Make sure you tell Genesis I said congratulations."

"Of course, I will. The gift I'm getting will

also be from the both of us."

"I already knew that," Chantal remarked as if T-Roc telling her was unnecessary. "Have you spoken to Justina?" she questioned moving on to another subject. I wanted to know when she's coming home."

"I spoke to her the other day. She mentioned Aaliyah's engagement party is coming up. Not sure if she's coming home afterwards or if she's staying until the wedding."

"Maybe I should take a trip to Miami. I feel like I haven't seen our daughter in forever. I really miss her."

"I miss her too. I'm also concerned," T-Roc revealed.

"Concerned? She's there with Aaliyah what do you have to be concerned about?"

T-Roc had been debating ever since he got the news whether or not he should discuss this with his wife. Up until now he decided not to but lately he'd been itching to share his concerns. But the person he confided in had to be someone who wouldn't use the information against his daughter. Chantal was the obvious choice.

"Did Justina ever mention dating a guy named Markell?"

Chantal stood fidgeting with the latch on

her bra as if trying to recall if the name sounded familiar. "Nope," she finally said tossing the bra down on the marble bathroom floor and slipping out of her satin panties.

"When I was helping Lorenzo deal with a situation regarding Genesis, I met up with a man and he said Justina came to Philly a few times with a guy named Markell. He said they were a couple."

"Maybe the man was mistaken," Chantal shrugged, wishing T-Roc would get to the point so she could take her shower.

"He was positive and after I did some investigating of my own, she was involved with him."

"Okay, let's just say Justina was seeing this Markell guy, what's the big deal?"

"Markell was doing business with Arnez. Arnez was working with Maya. We know Arnez was trying to bring down Genesis and it's no secret Maya wanted to bring harm to Precious and Aaliyah."

"What are you saying, T-Roc!" Chantal had quickly become highly agitated.

"What if our daughter was somehow involved with..."

"With what?!" Chantal yelled, cutting her

husband off. "What are you accusing Justina of?"

"Markell is dead, Chantal." T-Roc's voice had now also taken an angry tone. "A man that our daughter was dating, who she never told us about. He was doing business with Arnez and Justina was making trips to Philly with him as not only his girlfriend but his partner in business. Something isn't adding up."

"Now you're saying our daughter is a murderer? You can't be serious." Chantal slit her eyes at T-Roc. "What...you think Justina killed this Markell guy?" Chantal was waiting for her husband to say hell no but instead he said.

"Maybe so." T-Roc sighed putting his hands behind his head. "When too many things don't add up, it means something is wrong."

"Yeah, something is wrong with you. How dare you make such cruel accusations about our daughter!"

"Is it so farfetched, Chantal? I mean really. You shot and killed Sway Stone and almost killed our daughter in the process, mistaking her for Aaliyah. Let's not forget about Andre and Tyler, when you tried to run them over with your car." T-Roc shook his head.

"Oh, so now our daughter being a potential killer is all my fault. Like you're a fuckin' saint!"

Chantal shot back.

"We both know I'm far from a saint. That being said, with your DNA and mine, it's even more plausible Justina is a killer. The only question now is, what do we do about it?"

"I refuse to believe my beautiful baby girl is capable of what you're saying."

"I understand. Initially, I felt the same way but I've never lived my life being afraid of the truth. If our daughter has been involved in some shady shit, I'll get to the bottom of it," T-Roc stated assertively.

"Then what?" Chantal asked.

"I'll make sure Justina's protected and nothing leads back to her. Then we'll have to figure out how to get our daughter the help she needs because being a killer ain't gon' cut it."

"Delondo followed my advice and reached out to Genesis. Well not Genesis but one of his partners who is cool with him. The Lorenzo guy I told you about," Astrid told Arnez.

"Very good." Arnez grinned in delight. "I have a feeling my plan is going to come together perfectly."

"You better hope this Caleb dude is ready because Delondo also told me he's meeting with Lorenzo tonight. He's coming to Philly."

"Impressive. I wasn't expecting for Genesis and his partners to move this quickly. They're not wasting any time."

"No, they're not. It doesn't give you much time to prep Caleb."

"Don't worry about him, Astrid. Caleb is a young and very hungry soldier. There's a reason I chose to make him the new king of Philly."

"You better be right because I think this will be your last chance to bring down Genesis. If we mess this up, there won't be a second chance."

"Don't you think I know this. If Maya hadn't been so fixated on killing Aaliyah things would be completely different right now. Aaliyah's the only reason Supreme got involved. Once that happened, everything imploded. He killed Emory, he set out to find Talisa and you know the rest." Arnez balled up his fist becoming consumed with rage.

"Relax. My intent wasn't to upset you. I only wanted to stress how important it was to get it right this time."

"Trust me, I'm well aware. That's why I decided to go a different route. Team up with someone who has no family attachments to anyone I'm trying to take down. Caleb doesn't have a dog in this fight. He's only fighting to bring his brother home from jail. I can help with that and in return he helps me. I say it's a win/win relationship."

"It sounds promising but like I expressed from the jump, Caleb's age is troubling for me. He's a teenager and we both know how impulsive they can be. I'm not sold on the idea of him leading the way."

"Caleb won't be leading shit. I will! All he'll be doing is following my instructions and trust me he will."

"How can you be so sure?"

"Because I found his weakness. He loves his family. A man who loves their family, will do anything to protect them."

"You might be right," Astrid agreed.

"I know I'm right. All I need is for my lovely little sister to continue doing her part and I'll finally give Genesis the payback he's due very soon."

"You always looked out for me and our mother, so whatever you need me to do, I'm all in. My loyalty runs deep for you."

Astrid leaned in and held Arnez's hand. Seeing her once handsome brother with burns all over his body, including a part of his face, made her cringe. He was now able to walk on his own, feed himself, and overall was doing much better health wise but he would never be the same again.

"Astrid, you're the only person I trust. You've proven your allegiance to my cause and you will be rewarded for your devotion," Arnez vowed.

Chapter Seven

Invisible Enemy

Lorenzo and Amir entered the upscale restaurant in the Rittenhouse Square neighborhood to meet with Delondo and Khyree. Lorenzo reserved a private dining room, thinking that an expensive meal and a swanky ambiance would put the men in a more compromising mood.

"Both of you are right on time," Lorenzo said pleased. "This meeting is starting off the way I like." Lorenzo shook both of their hands followed by Amir before they all sat down.

"Before we order anything, we need to address this situation since it's the reason for our visit," Amir stated.

"I agree," Lorenzo nodded. "Delondo, since you reached out to me regarding your concerns, why don't you speak on the matter first."

Delondo bobbed his head in Lorenzo and Amir's direction, before resting his eyes on Khyree, who was wearing a smug smirk on his face. Dude rubbed Delondo the wrong way. He remembered when Khyree was trying to make a come up. He was barely getting by. He even tried to get a member of Delondo's team to recruit him but nobody was feeling his arrogant attitude. Even when Khyree was broke he had a superiority complex. Now that he was running shit in Philly his boldness was on ten.

"As both of you know I had to chill for a minute and let things die down."

Lorenzo and Amir both nodded their heads knowing Delondo was referring to him having someone in his crew that was snitching to the feds.

"While my team was playin' it low, someone stepped in and started taking over sections I supply."

"Man, you know that someone is me," Khyree jumped in and said like he was proud to be the offender.

"I was trying not to jump to conclusions but since you owning up to the shit."

"We wouldn't be here having this fuckin' meeting if everybody in this room didn't know it was me," Khyree scoffed, flipping away the napkin in front of him.

"Nigga, if you..."

"Both of you hold up!" Lorenzo pounded his fist down on the table before Delondo could finish his sentence. "We not here for this. This meeting is about solutions not a bunch of unnecessary bickering."

Delondo and Khyree both frowned up their faces. Neither wanted to hear the shit Lorenzo was spewing but felt like they didn't have a choice in the matter.

"Khyree, you get a lot of product from us but my father has a great deal of respect for Delondo," Amir spoke up and said.

"Same here," Delondo wanted to make clear.

"For that reason, we want to squash any potential beef between the two of you before things turn ugly. The solution to that would be for you to maintain your territories Khyree and Delondo you continue to run yours."

"Sounds fair to me," Lorenzo chimed in agreeing with Amir.

"You know I'm in. That's all I wanted in the first place," Delondo stated.

The three men turned their attention to Khyree who seemed more interested in browsing over the wine list then giving input to the conversation.

"I guess we're all in agreement then," Lorenzo said standing up.

"Hold up! Caleb is bringing in a ton of paper off those new spots. It's not really my problem that you had to fall back and left an opening to be taken over," Khyree shrugged.

Delondo was about to respond but Amir put his index finger up, signaling for him to wait a minute. "First off, who is Caleb?" Amir asked.

"He's one of my best workers if not the best," Khyree replied. "He's managed to make those spots into some of my top earners. I tell you what, Delondo. Let Caleb keep running those locations and I'll toss a couple of mine yo' way." Khyree lightly rubbed his pencil styled mustache. Obviously, he used trimmers on a daily to maintain the simple above the lip line look.

"Who the fuck you think you talkin' too."

Delondo barked. "You a disrespectful fuck boy."

"Nigga what!"

"You heard what I fuckin' said. You ain't gon' toss me shit. You gon' give me back my territories or I'ma take them shits back," Delondo warned.

"That won't be necessary, Delondo." Lorenzo's tone was calm trying to bring about a cease-fire. "Khyree is going to make sure his worker Caleb, stops moving product in those areas ASAP. Aren't you, Khyree?"

Khyree sucked his teeth like the song 'I can't hear you' was playing.

"No doubt Khyree is gonna get his man outta Delondo's territory, or he will need to find another supplier because he won't be gettin' shit from us," Amir proclaimed.

That statement got Khyree's attention. "You can't tell me where to move my product. Once I buy it, I can supply to who the fuck I want!" Khyree declared.

"True you can. But we also have the right to decline providing you with such product," Amir shot back.

"All the money I put in ya's pocket, you would cut me off to appease this nigga?!" Khyree mocked.

"Believe or not, Khyree, everything in this

business ain't about money," Lorenzo said.

"Whatever, everything is 'bout that dollar." Khyree shook his head.

"Some things are about having mutual re-spect," Amir asserted. "There is more than enough money to be made in the streets of Philly, so there is no need for a war to break out over some bullshit."

Khyree wanted to stick his middle finger up and say fuck you to all three of them. The reason he didn't was because he couldn't beat their prices or the quality of their drugs. He would only be fucking himself. So, for now he had to play along until a better situation presented itself.

"A'ight, ya win. Delondo, you can have yo' spots back."

"Great! This is good news. Now, let's eat." Lorenzo clapped his hands, pleased everything got settled.

"I know what I'm having," Delondo smiled.

"Me too," Amir chimed in.

"What about you?" Lorenzo asked.

"I lost my appetite." Khyree grabbed his car keys from the table and walked out the private dining room, not saying another word.

"I'll go speak to him." Amir got up from the table before Lorenzo stopped him.

"Let him go. Khyree pissed right now but he'll get over it," Lorenzo reassured him. "Now let's eat."

"Caleb, are you ready for what's about to go down?" Arnez asked.

"You still haven't told me what that is."

"Before I do, I need to make sure you're all in. This isn't something you can waver on. If you're not all in, this is the time to let me know."

"What about my brother? He only has a court appointed attorney right now. I need to get him a real lawyer, so he can at least get out on bail," Caleb made clear. "I need more than your word."

Arnez stood up and walked over to a coat closet in the hallway entrance. He disappeared for a couple minutes and returned holding a black leather briefcase. Arnez placed it on the glass top cocktail table.

"What's in that?" Caleb questioned.

"Open it." Arnez leaned back on the sofa. "This should validate my word."

"Damn." Was all Caleb could say. He had never in his life seen that amount of cash. "This is for me?"

"Yes. I believe it's more than enough to retain any lawyer you want and money for bail with a little left over."

Caleb gawked at the stacks of money for a few more seconds before closing the briefcase. He knew every dollar in there came with long strings attached. He wanted to walk away and not make a deal with the devil but then images of his mother, niece, and brother flashed through his head. There was a sharp pain nudging him to say no but he had more than himself to think about.

"I'm all in," Caleb confirmed.

"Good. Listen carefully because what you do next, will decide your fate." Arnez leaned forward and began to breakdown how his devious plan would unfold.

Chapter Eight

Actin' Up

"Baby, hi," Talisa said smiling when she answered Genesis's call.

"Hello, beautiful. I'm missing you. Can't wait to see your face."

"That will be very soon as our dinner reservation is at seven o'clock. Is Amir meeting us there or is he coming here and we're going to ride together."

"Amir had to go to Philly and handle some

business," Genesis said.

"Oh, that's too bad. I was looking forward to spending time with my two favorite men. Instead of a family dinner it will be a romantic one. Just the two of us."

"About that." Genesis hesitated for a moment but then continued. "Skylar and the baby got released from the hospital today, so I'm getting them settled in. I'll try not to stay too long but I need to reschedule our dinner date tonight."

"I see."

"Talisa, please don't be upset. I promise to make it up to you."

"I understand. When will I be able to meet your baby? I know she's beautiful. Have you had a chance to talk to Skylar about what I said?"

"The day I did, she went into labor. But I'ma make it happen," Genesis assured her. "Thank you for being so understanding. You truly are the best wife any man could ever want."

"It's called being in love," Talisa replied sweetly. But there was nothing sweet about how she was feeling. Talisa had been stuck on an island for many years but the hot sun hadn't fried her brain. She knew exactly what Skylar was up to. Skylar was going to use their baby to keep Genesis by her side as much as possible, hoping he would fall back in love with her and they would be a happy family. But Talisa had her own plans. She would welcome Genesis's baby into their home and Genevieve would be a part of their family. Skylar would either accept her role as the mother of his child or run the risk of being an outsider.

"I'm in love with you too. Now and forever," Genesis told his wife. "I'll be home soon."

"Who were you talking to?" Skylar asked when Genesis got off the phone.

"I was talking to Talisa."

"Oh. Look at Genevieve, she's waking up from her nap." Skylar walked over to Genesis and put the baby in his arms. "Isn't she beautiful."

"She really is." Genesis sat down on the couch, cradling his daughter. Her body was warm and soft. Her face was angelic. Holding her felt almost healing to him.

"I'm sure Talisa is ready for you to get home, so it's okay if you have to go."

"She understands that I want to spend time with my daughter."

"That's kind of her."

"Talisa has always had a beautiful heart. She really wants to be a part of our daughter's life. I know Genevieve has probably been all you've had time to think about but have you decided when Talisa can come over to talk to you and see our baby?"

"Honestly, I haven't had time to think about it," Skylar replied, doing her best to conceal her uneasiness.

"Genevieve is a newborn, so little," Genesis smiled, touching her tiny hand. "I think it's much too soon for her to leave the house, so since I can't bring her home with me yet, I think the best option is to have Talisa come over here."

It was obvious to Skylar that Genesis wasn't letting up. He would be persistent until she gave in. She realized it would be unwise to come across as the bitter baby mama, especially since Talisa always appeared to be the poster child for sainthood.

"Of course, Talisa can come over and see Genevieve. She's your wife and should be a part of our daughter's life."

"Skylar, thank you." Genesis was surprised and relieved she was willing to oblige his request without putting up a fight.

"You sound stunned. Did you think I would object?"

"I wasn't sure how you would react given we were discussing Talisa right before you went into labor."

"My hormones were all over the place then. Now that I've given birth and I can see my feet again," she giggled. "I'm in a better mood. Although the moment my doctor gives me the okay, I'll be working out so I can lose the rest of this baby weight."

"Skylar, don't be hard on yourself. You look beautiful."

"Thanks, but when you get on social media and all these women have this amazing snapback, it becomes extremely stressful," Skylar sighed.

"You can't pay that stuff any attention. I'm not on social media but Amir is and he tells me all that garbage is fake. He swears most of the women Photoshop and filter themselves to the point their own mother wouldn't recognize them." Genesis and Skylar both laughed.

"You've made me feel a lot better. Thank you but I'm still ready to get back into my favorite jeans."

"And you will. Like I said, I think you look great but how you feel about yourself is what matters. I tell you what. Once you reach your post baby weight goal, you can go on a shopping spree, my treat."

"Are you serious?" Skylar asked excitedly.

"Yes. It's the least I can do for you bringing

this beautiful baby girl into the world."

"You've given me just the motivation I needed," she beamed.

Skylar gazed at Genesis holding their child with love in her eyes. What Genesis thought was a simple gesture of gratitude, Skylar took it as a sign there was hope for them to rekindle their relationship. His kindness renewed Skylar's determination to win her baby daddy back.

Lorenzo, Amir, and Delondo enjoyed a good meal, and some colorful conversation over drinks. By the time they left the restaurant, all three were feeling nice and tipsy, but luckily they had drivers to take them to their destinations.

"Man, it was good hanging out wit' ya," Delondo said giving Lorenzo and Amir dap as they waited for their cars to pull up. "And I appreciate both of you steppin' up for me regarding the Khyree situation. Won't neva forget that."

"No doubt. We all out here gettin' money. There has to be a level of respect out here in these streets if we want to keep it that way," Lorenzo stated.

"I feel you on that." Delondo nodded.

"Lorenzo, I think that's our ride coming now," Amir commented seeing what appeared to be a black Yukon truck pulling up. "He need to turn those high beam lights off. That shit fuckin' wit' my vision."

Within seconds of Amir making his comment all hell broke loose. The back passenger window of the Yukon rolled down and the only sound you heard was bullets spraying. It seemed inevitable a bloodbath would be what was left in front of the upscale restaurant. The men were scrambling to find refuge but they were completely taken off guard, so all they could do was pray and fall to the ground in hopes they would miss being shot.

Amir appeared to be like a deer caught in the headlights. He stood frozen for a moment and could see the barrel of the gun pointed in his direction. His life flashed before him. He was positive this was about to be his last moment on earth. He would never see a loved one again. In those brief seconds, his mind fixated on his mother. He thanked God that although it was brief, he was able to spend time with the woman who gave him life and loved him unconditionally. He closed his eyes as if embracing his fate. Then he felt this powerful force that seemed to literally sweep him off his feet. For a moment Amir thought he had been shot but he didn't feel any pain, only a slight discomfort from his body hitting the ground. There was this heavy weight that seemed to be pinning him down and when he opened his eyes, he realized it was a man.

"Amir! Amir! Are you okay?!" Lorenzo called out running towards him.

"What tha fuck!" Delondo barked standing up, trying to wrap his mind around what just happened. He then noticed Lorenzo standing over Amir and some other guy who were on the ground. 'Yo, Amir ain't get shot did he?!"

Lorenzo moved the body that was on top of Amir and saw blood. "Oh shit! Amir, you been hit!"

"Nah, it ain't my blood," Amir mumbled. "Who is that? He saved my life," he wanted to know looking down at the guy who took a bullet meant for him.

"I don't know but Delondo, call 911! We need to get this man to the hospital," Lorenzo shouted. They weren't sure how badly he was hurt but they saw blood which meant he needed medical attention.

"The ambulance should be here any minute," Delondo told them after getting off the phone.

"I swear, I bet that motherfucker Khyree was behind this shit! I'ma kill that nigga. He a dead man!"

Chapter Nine

It Wasn't Me

"Astrid, I was just about to call you," Arnez said letting his sister in.

"After Delondo called me, I came right over. He's furious. He thinks Khyree tried to have him, Lorenzo, and Amir killed tonight."

"Then that means my planned worked," Arnez smiled.

"That was you who ordered the hit? When I told you where Delondo was having his meeting,

I wasn't expecting for you to try to kill him!" Astrid yelled.

"Calm down. Nobody was supposed to die."

"If you have someone spraying bullets in front of a restaurant, what else do you think is gonna happen," she snapped.

"Call it an epic performance."

"Arnez, can you please stop talking in riddles and tell me why you had someone shoot at my husband tonight."

"Have a seat and calm down," Arnez told Astrid while pouring her a glass of wine.

"I'm calm now, so please tell me what the hell is going on."

"This is why I didn't want to tell you what was going on until after it happened," Arnez said handing her the glass of wine. "I didn't want you getting yourself all worked up for no reason."

Astrid quickly gulped her wine down growing impatient. She loved her brother and would do anything for him but although she was betraying Delondo by working with Arnez, Astrid loved her husband too.

"I'm listening, Arnez," she said waiting for him to tell her what was going on.

"I didn't realize how emotionally invested you are in Delondo," Arnez commented. "I hope that won't interfere with you helping me."

"I've always had your back and that won't change but Delondo is Delilah's father. I don't want him dead. That wasn't part of our agreement."

"True and that's not part of the plan. I simply needed a way to get rid of Khyree and bring Caleb into the fold."

"I get that part but how does it coincide with my husband being shot at?"

"I'm sure things are a bit chaotic at the moment, so Delondo probably didn't have a chance to tell you someone took a bullet for Amir tonight."

"No, he didn't. He just said Khyree had someone shoot at them while they were outside of the restaurant. He told me he was fine but had to handle some business and would call me later on."

"Well, you'll soon find out that Caleb was the one who saved Amir's life although he was never in any danger. But now Caleb looks like a hero and Khyree appears to be the enemy."

"So, wait, no one actually got shot?"

"No one was supposed to get shot but Caleb did end up having to take a bullet which made it appear even more like an authentic hit. But my men were under strict instructions not to shoot to kill."

"That's a bit risky. How did you get Caleb to agree to that?"

"My men are professionals. Initially Caleb was reluctant but I assured him he wouldn't be in any real danger. Plus, he received a substantial amount of money. I wanted to show him my intentions are good."

"Arnez, I don't know if you're a genius, crazy, or just lucky but that's one brilliant plan. Khyree is now good as dead and Caleb has set himself up to be put in the perfect position to take his place."

"I would say I'm a combination of all three and thank you. I'm rather proud at how lovely my plan is unfolding."

"You're also a great judge of people. I would've never thought Caleb had enough heart to carry this out. He's much tougher than he appears to be. I definitely underestimated him," Astrid admitted.

"Yes. That young man has the potential to be one of the great ones. I'll have to keep a close eye on him."

Arnez was always confident Caleb was the right person to pull off his latest stunt but even he had to admit he underestimated him. He wasn't the mindless young puppet he could easily manipulate. There was a burgeoning warrior inside of Caleb waiting to take over the world.

"Now that we know the dude who saved Amir's life is gonna be a'ight, me and my men 'bout to track Khyree's snake ass down," Delondo told Lorenzo.

"Hold up on that," Lorenzo told him.

"Why tha fuck would I do that. We could've all died tonight!" Delondo fumed.

"I know that but we're not positive it was Khyree."

"Yo, you can't be serious!" Delondo threw his hands up in the air like Lorenzo sounded crazy. "Who tha fuck else knew we were there? Nobody but Khyree's punk ass."

"True but..."

"But nothing!"

"Delondo, all I'm asking is you hold off for a minute."

"And give that nigga another chance to kill me? Hell no! What about you and Amir...he coulda killed ya too!" Delondo added.

"Give me twenty-four hours. That's all I'm asking for. I just want a chance to speak with Khyree. See what he has to say," Lorenzo explained.

"What, you think that nigga gon' admit he tried to have us killed?" Delondo gave Lorenzo the, 'I know you ain't that dumb' stare.

"Trust me. If Khyree is lying, the truth will come out. Remember, I stepped up for you tonight. All I'm asking is for a little time to get the truth."

"Twenty-four hours, Lorenzo. That's all I'm giving you. After that, Khyree is a dead man." Delondo stormed off and Lorenzo shook his head, wondering why Khyree would make such a reckless move. If in fact it was him.

"Delondo broke out in a rage like he was on his way to kill a muthafucka. I'm assuming that muthafucka gotta be Khyree," Amir said, walking up on Lorenzo.

"He was planning to but I told him to hold off."

"Why you do that?" Amir's face had a grimaced expression on it.

"I get all signs point to Khyree being responsible but I don't wanna rush to judgment. Trying to kill us would guarantee him a death sentence. He ain't a stupid nigga."

"Yeah but he is an arrogant one," Amir reminded Lorenzo. "If the hit happened as Khyree planned, then none of us would be alive to seek retribution. So, the death sentence he was guaranteed to receive would've never come to fruition. Dead men can't talk."

"You making valid points but something don't feel right. I don't think Khyree is good for this. I might be wrong. I'm 'bout to go speak with him. Delondo is only willing to wait twenty-four hours before making his move."

"You 'bout to go have a conversation wit' the nigga who tried to take us out. Come on, Lorenzo. That don't make no sense."

"I have a few shooters in Philly I'ma bring wit' me."

"Well, I'm coming too."

"No. You stay here, Amir. I need to speak to Khyree alone. We have history. I'll get a better read from him if he doesn't have his guard up. If we go in there tag teaming the nigga, I won't find out shit."

"I'll wait here while you speak with, Khyree."

"You're not heading back to the hotel?"

"Not right now. I wanna speak to the dude that saved my life before I leave. Once the doctor and nurse come out his room, I'll go in," Amir said.

"Okay. I'll call you after I speak with Khyree so we can decide what our next move will be."

"Cool," Amir nodded.

Watching Lorenzo as he made his exit, Amir couldn't grasp why he just didn't let Delondo kill Khyree. There wasn't a doubt in his mind Khyree was the one behind the hit. Amir felt at this point, Lorenzo was simply prolonging the inevitable. Khyree was a dead man.

"Lorenzo, I wasn't expecting to see you again tonight. Did you come to apologize for makin' me look like a chump tonight?" Khyree scoffed.

One of Lorenzo's people gave him the head's up that Khyree was at a small corner bar he owned. He figured popping up unexpectedly, catching Khyree off guard, would be the best way to approach him.

"Do you mind if I have a seat?" Lorenzo's cool, laidback tone put Khyree at ease.

"You the boss. You can sit wherever you like." Khyree had the bartender pour him another drink as Lorenzo sat down on the bar stool next to him." A couple hours after you left the restaurant, somebody tried to kill us." Lorenzo said casually." Damn, it's a good thing I left early...huh." Khyree shook the ice in his glass and softly chuckled.

"You think that's funny? We almost died tonight."

"But you didn't 'cause if you had, you wouldn't be sittin' right next to me now, would you?"

Lorenzo wasn't sure if Khyree's flippant attitude was him being his typical overconfident self, or if he was doing his best to make it seem he had nothing to hide. Surly if Khyree was the one responsible for ordering the hit, he would at least pretend to be concerned or would he. Lorenzo was having a difficult time coming up with the answer for that.

"Khyree, I'ma be straight wit' you like I've always been. Delondo and Amir believe you're the one who ordered the hit on us. I'm trying to give you the benefit of the doubt. I mean I was the one who put you on and brought you to Genesis to move product in Philly. I would hate to find out you shitted on me."

"Man, you know I ain't had shit to do wit' it. If you believed for a second I was the one who set that shit up, you wouldn't be here talkin' to me. I would be dead," Khyree said matter of factly.

"Look me in my eye and give me your word you had nothing to do with what went down tonight." Lorenzo's stare was so intense, it would make a motherfucker scared to even blink.

"Word on my dead mother, may she rest in peace, I ain't have nothin' to do wit' that hit."

"Say no more. I believe you." Lorenzo did believe Khyree too. Because if he was lying, Lorenzo felt he had to be the best liar to ever cross his path.

"Good. Now you can go tell Delondo to get off my dick!" Khyree retorted nodding at the bartender to fill up his glass one more time.

Chapter Ten

The Set Up

Amir woke up extra early because he wanted to make it to the hospital before the man who saved his life was discharged. By the time the doctor and nurse had cleared his room last night, the man had fallen asleep. Now Amir was back and wasn't leaving until he was able to tell the man thank you.

"Looks like you on track to make a full recovery," Amir commented when he entered the hospital room. "Either that food taste better than it looks or you hungry," he laughed.

"Not hungry, more like starving."

"I'm Amir and you are?"

"Caleb."

"Caleb, I'm honored to meet you."

"Honored!" Caleb's face frowned out.

"I'm the reason you in that hospital bed right now. You saved my life. So, yes I'm honored."

"Thank you, but I couldn't stand there and watch you die."

"But you really could've, instead you took a bullet for me. I'm hoping I can return the favor and do something for you too."

"Do something like what?" Caleb asked.

"Besides covering all your medical bills, I wanna do something that will benefit your life. I mean you look mad young. You still in school?"

"Nah. I dropped out a couple years ago. School ain't for me. I'm tryna be more of the entrepreneur type."

"I feel you. So, are you currently employed?"

"Of course, how else I'ma eat?" Caleb glared at Amir as if saying, *dumb fuck, shit ain't free.*

"Where do you work?" Amir asked.

"Why do you care?" Caleb shot back.

"Because you're brave and I respect that. We

need more people like you on these streets."

"Thanks, but I was only doing what I felt was right. Are the other two dudes okay?"

"Lorenzo and Delondo are fine."

"I'm glad to hear that, but yeah I do have a job."

"Cool, but so you know, if you ever need to be put to work, let me know. I have a lot of connects in Philly. I also wanted to give you this." Amir tossed down an envelope full of money on the tray Caleb was using to eat his breakfast.

"Man, I can't take yo' money." Caleb handed the envelope back to Amir.

"I wanna do something for you."

"Then watch yo' back." Caleb warned

"By the look in your eyes, that seems like more than some friendly advice. Is there something you need to tell me?" Amir asked. "If so, you should speak up now."

"That's some bullshit!" Delondo roared, slamming down the phone.

"Baby, what's wrong?" Astrid ran into her husband's office and asked, hearing the anger in his voice from the other room.

"I just got off the phone with Lorenzo. Khyree swear he had nothing to do wit' us being shot at last night and Lorenzo believes him. I know that nigga responsible though." Delondo clenched up his fist, wishing he could put it down Khyree's throat.

"What are you going to do?"

"I can't do shit. I gave Lorenzo my word I wouldn't touch Khyree. If I go back on it, I'm asking for all hell to break loose. I'm not interested in starting a war I can't win." Delondo was seething. Astrid had never seen her husband so upset.

"Babe, you need to calm down. Getting yourself worked up isn't going to help."

"I'm sick of that arrogant mutherfucka!" he pounded down his fist on top of his desk. "His slick ass always gettin' away wit' some shit. It's gon' catch up to his ass eventually and I hope I'm right there to get a front row view."

"Where are you going?" Astrid questioned after Delondo stood up and grabbed his keys.

"I'll be back in a couple hours. I need to speak to my crew." Delondo gave his wife a quick kiss on the cheek and left. She waited until she saw him drive away and then called Arnez.

"Good afternoon!" Arnez answered in a rather upbeat voice.

"You sound like you're in a good mood," Astrid remarked.

"Why wouldn't I be, everything is going according to plan."

"I wouldn't celebrate just yet. Delondo left out of here furious. Khyree denied being behind the hit, and Lorenzo believes him. He made Delondo promise to leave Khyree alone."

"I'm sure Lorenzo did. But no worries, I expected Khyree to deny it, since it's true," Arnez laughed.

"But if Lorenzo has made Khyree untouchable how is that going to help you? Your plan now becomes useless."

"Astrid, you have so much to learn. Just sit back, follow my lead and watch how this all plays out. My lunch is ready, I'll call you later."

Astrid stood dumbfounded when she got off the phone with her brother. She was basic at best when it came to scheming compared to Arnez. He was devious, evil but very smart. Astrid's biggest goal in life had been reached by simply marrying a rich man like Delondo. That was the extent of where her manipulating went. It was only because of her undying loyalty to her brother that Arnez had any real use for you. He was the puppeteer and Astrid was one of his many puppets.

"Caleb, I'ma ask you again, is there something you wanna tell me?"

"All I'ma say is be careful. Especially when you here in Philly. I've already said enough."

"I'ma ask you a question and I want you to be honest with me." Amir had a hunch and wanted to see if he was correct.

"What is it?"

"Do you know who shot at us last night?"

Caleb's body tensed up and he had an uncomfortable look on his face.

"If you know, you can tell me," Amir pressed.

"No, I can't because if I do, I'ma dead man. I shouldn't have saved your life in the first place."

"Why did you then?"

"Because your father is well respected in these streets and I didn't think his people should go out like that."

"You know my father?"

"I've never met him but every hustler and wannabe hustler in Philly heard of Genesis."

"I assume you deal then, who do you work for?"

"Man, if I tell you that then I'm telling on

myself. I ain't stupid. Like I said, I already done more than I should've. But you alive and so are the two other men you were with. Let's leave it at that."

"I can't do that, Caleb. Somebody tried to kill us. Whoever it is, has to be dealt with."

"I'm supposed to risk putting my own life in danger again and my livelihood. A nigga got to eat."

"You don't have to worry about that. Not only will I make sure you're protected, I'll also make sure you get supplied whatever you need directly from me. You can be your own boss."

"I don't know, Amir. This game is treacherous. What if you can't get to him and he finds out it was me who not only saved your life but also ratted him out." Caleb shook his head like he was torn but he wasn't. He was staying on script, slightly improvising to add his own personal touch.

"You have my word and I speak for my father when I say you will be rewarded for your cooperation."

Caleb continued to hesitate. Not easily caving to Amir's request which made him appear even more believable. If he didn't have dreams of becoming the next drug kingpin, he could easily make it as a Hollywood actor.

"You sure this won't link back to me? I'm not only takin' my life into consideration but my family too."

"Caleb, you have my word. Now tell me who orchestrated this hit?"

"The nigga I work for. His name is Khyree. He's the one who sent those shooters to take ya out."

"You did the right thing by telling me, Caleb. Thank you."

"I hope you don't make me regret this shit."

"You won't. This is probably one of the best decisions you've ever made in your life. Fuck Khyree. You 'bout to be on to bigger and better things. I can promise you that, Caleb."

Chapter Eleven

Greenlight

T-Roc had made the trip to the Divine Care treatment center in Costa Mesa, California in search of answers. Before confronting Justina, he wanted to be amply loaded with all the facts. The luxury facility had a beach community feel. They offered holistic therapy that was supposed to treat patients in the context of their entire lives and health status. They also gave individualized treatment that was customized on a person's unique needs and circumstances. It mixed one on one therapy with yoga, addiction education, music, and literary therapy. The peaceful retreat seemed like the ideal place for someone to heal their body, mind and soul.

A couple of years ago, Justina seemed to be in a very dark place. No matter what T-Roc and Chantal did, they couldn't pull her from under the gloomy cloud that seemed to follow her. Pretty soon she became so distant, T-Roc was afraid he was about to lose his daughter forever. Determined not to let that happen, he decided to send Justina to Divine Care. It was a highly reputable treatment center that treated patients with a different variety of issues. Initially Justina refused to go but once T-Roc threatened to financially cut her off she finally agreed. At first, Justina wasn't making any progress. She followed all the rules and attended her therapy classes but she seemed to be going through the motions. Then one day there seemed to be a breakthrough. For the first time in what seemed like forever, Justina was motivated to come out of her shell and start living life again. T-Roc and Chantal were both thrilled to have their once happy daughter back but now T-Roc had to wonder if that was all a facade.

"Thank you for seeing me on such short notice," T-Roc said to the facility director before taking a seat.

"It's my pleasure. What can I do for you? You mentioned you had some questions about your daughter Justina. I did pull her file, although you're aware we have a strict privacy policy when it comes to our patients?"

"Yes, I'm aware of that but I'm interested in getting a record of any visitors my daughter might've had during her stay here."

"We can't give out that information either unless we have the patient's consent. Justina would have to authorize the release."

"Mrs. Blaylock, I grasp you want to protect the privacy of your patients but this is my daughter. Furthermore, I paid for her treatment and let's not forget, I made a substantial donation due to the success she had here," T-Roc reminded the facility's director.

"Divine Care truly appreciates all of our donors especially the ones who have made a significant donation such as yourself but..."

"And who plans to make another donation," T-roc jumped in, pulling out his checkbook.

Mrs. Blaylock's eyes lit up. Divine Care was a private facility so she more than welcomed sizeable donations. She also reasoned sharing private information with a previous patient's parent would be harmless. But to cover her ass, she went for a subtler approach.

"I need to speak with one of our therapists. I'll be gone for about ten minutes," Mrs. Blaylock said taking Justina's file from her drawer and placing it on top of her desk. "I'm sure you'll be able to find everything you need while I'm gone and as always we greatly appreciate the donation." She smiled before closing her office door.

T-Roc grabbed the folder but instead of going through each document, he pulled out his iPhone and took pictures. He wasn't expecting to get access to all of Justina's files but now that he had, he wanted to take his time and read through them carefully. Not only did he want to see who had visited his daughter but he also wanted to find out if Justina was as troubled as he suspected.

"You didn't say shit about me catchin' a bullet!" Caleb barked at Arnez. "I coulda got killed."

"I apologize, you weren't supposed to get shot but you were never in any danger. My men knew not to hurt you. If they wanted you dead then you would be dead."

"The doctor told me if that bullet had come two inches closer, it woulda hit a vital artery and I woulda bled out. Playin' wit' my life wasn't part of the deal!"

"Caleb, calm down. I get you upset and I can admit when I'm wrong. Because of my miscalculation, I've included a bonus for your trouble." Arnez walked off and reappeared with a few stacks of money. Caleb was starting to wonder if Arnez had a bank stashed back there.

"I think this should compensate you for your troubles." Arnez handed Caleb the money. "Have you heard anything else from Amir?" Arnez questioned, sitting back down.

"Not really. He told me to continue my regular work routine wit' Khyree and act like everything is normal," Caleb explained.

"They're strategically planning on making their move but it'll be happening soon. No way are they letting Khyree live too much longer. Just play your position and wait for Amir's call. I'll let you know how to handle him."

Caleb nodded his head as if listening to Arnez but he had no intentions of following his lead when it came to Amir. Caleb figured he would have better luck using his own instincts when dealing with him. He felt they had connected while at the hospital and Caleb planned on taking advantage of that.

"Lorenzo, what's the hold up with killing Khyree?" Amir questioned, pacing his hotel suite.

"I wanted to check out this kid Caleb. Make sure he was legit."

"He legitimately took a bullet for me. What else did you need to know?"

"If he really worked for Khyree. He could've been lying," Lorenzo scoffed.

"Was he?"

Lorenzo let out a deep sigh. "Unfortunately, not. He does work for Khyree. He has for a couple years now. Caleb's actually Khyree's biggest money maker."

"That's why his named sounded familiar. Khyree mentioned him in our meeting," Amir just remembered.

"Yeah, he did."

"Why do you sound disappointed?"

"Because I believed Khyree when he said he had nothing to do with the shooting. He stared me in my face and swore on his dead mother. I take shit like that personally. I vouched for Khyree. That nigga tried to kill us and probably plotting right now how to do it again, but this time get it right," Lorenzo fumed.

"Fuck that disrespectful prick. Get our best shooter on the phone, so we can get rid of Khyree's ass today!" Amir spit.

"It's already been handled," Lorenzo stood up and said. "I should be getting the call soon. Once I do, I'm heading back to New York. Your father wants you to stay here to oversee our territories. Since Khyree will no longer be around to move product, we have to make sure shit runs smoothly."

"At some point, we're going to need someone to step in and take Khyree's place. I can't stay in Philly forever."

"I know, just until you can find a replacement."

"I think I already have," Amir said.

"Who?"

"Caleb."

Lorenzo sat back down. "He's only seventeen. Don't you think Caleb's too young to be overseeing such a high volume of drugs?"

"No, I don't. Khyree said himself Caleb was

his biggest moneymaker. Yes, he's young, but clearly he has a lot of heart. He took a bullet for me didn't he?"

"Yeah, what he did was impressive and he has a lot of potential but Caleb is still a kid. I don't feel one hundred percent comfortable having a seventeen-year-old running our Philly territory. But Genesis has been wanting to give you more responsibilities, so I'll let you make the final decision regarding Caleb. Remember, if he succeeds or if he fails, it's all on you," Lorenzo asserted.

When Delondo approached the cemetery, he drove slowly and then pulled over to the side. He watched from a distance and noticed Khyree was in the exact location he was told he would be. Although it was the middle of the afternoon, due to the overcast the clouds were obscuring ninety-five percent of the sky, which brought about darkness. The gloomy atmosphere was the perfect precursor for what was about to unfold.

"I guess even someone as heartless as you, loves at least one person," Delondo said, sneaking up behind Khyree who was kneeling down.

"What the fuck are you doin' here?!"

"Is it appropriate for you to be using curse words while visiting your mother's gravesite?"

"You sonofabitch. Don't act like you give a fuck about what's appropriate when you come disrupting the personal time I'm spending wit' my mother. You don' lose yo' motherfuckin' mind." Khyree barked standing up.

"Slow down, son. You best stay over there where you at," Delondo warned.

"How the fuck you know where I was at anyway?"

"I got word from an extremely reliable source, you come visit your mother's gravesite every week on this exact day and time. I was also told, this is where you're most vulnerable because you always come alone. No henchman and unarmed."

"Hold up." Khyree put his hands in his pocket and started to laugh. "I know you didn't come here to kill me."

"This is a first. I've never seen a nigga laugh who was about to die," Delondo smirked.

"Die? That must mean you ready to die too. Because once Lorenzo finds out you killed me, you already know you next."

"The beautiful part of all this, Lorenzo gave

me the greenlight."

"You a fuckin' liar!" Khyree shouted.

"Nope. How do you think I came across the reliable source? He's done wit' you. He found out you were behind the hit."

"I ain't have nothin' to do wit' that shit! I told Lorenzo and he believed me. I don't know what the fuck is goin' on but once I get Lorenzo on the phone, he'll clear all this bullshit up," Khyree said pulling out his iPhone.

"Toss that shit down!" Delondo spit. "You ain't callin' Lorenzo. What part of done don't you get?!"

"Fuck you, Delondo! I'm callin' Lorenzo and it's gon' be yo' ass takin' a bullet!" he hollered back. But before Khyree could even click on contacts, Delondo pulled the trigger and blew off his hand.

Khyree's eyes widened in disbelief as he stared at his handless arm and the blood gushed out. His shock left him speechless.

"I told yo' stupid ass to toss the phone," Delondo mocked stepping closer to Khyree to finish him off. "I been waitin' for a reason to kill yo' punk ass. You been walkin' these streets, conducting reckless business 'cause you thought you couldn't be touched. The first rule you learn when you hustle, is that anybody can be gotten."

"I told you I didn't order that hit," Khyree mumbled through his excruciating pain.

"Whatever, nigga! I don't give a damn if you did or you didn't. Yo' ass need to go." Delondo released a succession of shots, riddling Khyree's body with bullets.

"Fuck you!" Khyree managed to mutter before falling to his death.

"Fuck you too. Now you have a resting place right next to yo' mama." Delondo spit on Khyree and walked away.

Chapter Twelve

Game Changer

Talisa was at the Oscar De La Renta boutique on Madison Avenue in search of a pair of shoes to go with a dress she had recently purchased, when she noticed a familiar face browsing the handbag section. At first, Talisa wavered on whether she should approach but she couldn't stop herself.

"Skylar, how are you?"

"Oh gosh, Talisa, you startled me!" Skylar jumped. "I didn't realize that was you. You cut your hair."

"Yes, I did. I wanted a change. It's just hair, it'll grow back but I'm actually enjoying this shorter cut."

"The cut compliments you. You look great," Skylar commented, noticing Talisa transformed from island girl to the personification of a Manhattan socialite since the last time the two women saw each other. She was wearing an off white Escada pantsuit with studding and black piping on the back, the sleeves and down the leg. Talisa completed her look with a pair of black Christian Louboutin pumps and a small leather clutch.

"Thank you," Talisa said politely. "Where's Genevieve, is she with the nanny?"

"Oh no, she's at the penthouse with my mother. I wanted to get out and do a little shopping since I've dropped most of my pregnancy weight. Genesis offered to hire a nanny but he's already been so good to me."

"I can see that," Talisa remarked curtly, being that Skylar was shopping at one of the priciest boutiques in Manhattan. She was positive it was on Genesis's dime.

"I hadn't planned on our first time seeing each other again would be out shopping but I'm glad I ran into you, Talisa. I wanted to apologize for leaving you on the island and taking so long to tell Genesis the truth. I was wrong and I hope one day you can forgive me." Skylar sounded sincere but Talisa didn't believe one word coming out of her mouth.

"I appreciate your apology but I understand why you did it and I don't blame you."

"Really?" Skylar asked looking confused by what Talisa said.

"Of course, I do. I would hate to give up a man like Genesis too. I would do anything necessary to hold on to him...anything," Talisa smiled.

Although Talisa didn't make any threats, Skylar could feel there was an underlying meaning to what her rival said.

"Thank you for accepting my apology."

"It's my pleasure. You know Genesis mentioned he wanted to have a small get together for close friends and family to celebrate the birth of his daughter."

"I didn't know that. He hasn't mentioned anything to me."

"I'm sure he will next time he comes to visit Genevieve. I told Genesis I would put everything together. Now that you've had your six-week checkup and Genevieve will be two months very soon, he thought it was the perfect time. I'm sure that won't be a problem for you. Would you like to have the get together at our place or yours?"

Talisa's question caught Skylar completely off guard and she felt obligated to accept Talisa's proposal.

"My place will be fine."

"Great. I'll call you later this week so we can set up a day for me to come over and discuss the plans," Talisa said taking out her phone. "Genesis will be thrilled when I tell him we were able to come to an agreement on this. Here, put in your contact information." Talisa handed her phone to Skylar, leaving her no other choice but to comply or say no which she didn't have the balls to do.

Talisa was irate on the inside but she stood watching Skylar with such poise and grace, no one would've had a clue of her true feelings. She needed to play hardball with her nemesis. Talisa had been trying to get Genesis to set up a day when she could go over and speak with Skylar but every single time, Skylar came up with some random excuse. Then she refused to allow Genesis to spend time with the baby at their place, once again always coming up with some excuse. Genesis didn't want to cause any waves because he believed the sweet, understanding baby mama act Skylar was performing with perfection. Talisa knew it was time she stepped in and shut the shit down once and for all.

"Hey pretty girl," Amir answered when he took Justina's call. "Are you missing me as much as I miss you?"

"You know I am. I can't wait for you to get to Miami."

"I can't wait for you to get back permanently to NYC so we can start looking for our crib together."

"Are you sure you're ready for us to start living together? That means no more bachelor pad for you," Justina teased.

"I can give all that up if it means you my official girl."

"Then after Aaliyah's wedding, we will be apartment hunting in the city. I have been enjoying the Miami weather and beaches but there's no place like New York. Plus, you're there."

"I feel the same way. NYC ain't the same without you. It would be nice to have your support right now anyway," Amir divulged.

"Is everything okay? You sounded a tad stressed."

"Between dealing with Caleb in Philly and making sure my mom's okay, it's been hectic."

"Is Caleb not working out the way you hoped?" Justina asked.

"Actually, he's doing fuckin' great. I still can't believe dude is only seventeen. The way he's so focused on business and making money, reminds me so much of my father, it's crazy. His grind had me spending a lot of time in Philly but we've gotten into a routine now, so I won't have to go there that much anymore."

"That's a good thing. What about your mother, you still think the baby situation is having a negative effect on your parent's marriage?"

"I do, even though neither one of them will admit it. My father is so attached to Genevieve. I understand it's his daughter but it's hard seeing how painful it is for my mother," Amir sadly admitted.

"Before your father continues doing all that bonding with the little girl, he needs to get a blood test. Unless he finally got one...did he?" Justina asked.

"No, not that I know of."

"What is your father waiting on? Please, we know how scandalous some chicks can be. Women be putting babies off on broke dudes, trust me, Skylar would lie, cheat, and steal if it meant Genesis would be her baby daddy. Maybe he is, but your father needs to get proof in the form of a DNA test," Justina stated. "But listen, I have to go. Aaliyah and Angel are waiting for me. I'll call you later. Love you."

"Love you too."

When Amir got off the phone with Justina he couldn't shake what she said. For his father's own protection, he needed to get a DNA test. What if ten years from now he found out Genevieve really wasn't his daughter. His father would be devastated. At least if he found out now, his heart might be broken but he could recover. Then what if it wasn't necessary for his parent's marriage to endure the stress of dealing with Skylar and her baby? If Genevieve wasn't his, then the problem would disappear just like that.

"Now all I have to do is convince my father to do a DNA test," Amir thought out loud while driving as he took the exit towards Philly.

"I still can't believe my baby is home," Ms. Ellis beamed hugging her son Prevan. "I was worried I would never be able to wrap my arms around you again," she cried.

"Well, I'm home now mama and you ain't never gotta worry about that again, thanks to my lil' brother," Prevan grinned.

"I got both of my boys now." Ms. Ellis pulled Caleb close for a group hug. "You did what I thought was the impossible," she said kissing Caleb on the cheek.

"Just glad I didn't let you down, ma," Caleb said relieved Arnez kept his word and his brother was finally home.

"Both of you stay right here," Ms. Ellis said when she heard the doorbell. "I think this is my surprise for you."

"Hi Grandma!" Amelia waved when Ms. Ellis opened the front door.

"Hey baby! Follow me. Grandma has a surprise for you." She didn't even bother greeting Celinda and her sister. Ms. Ellis took Amelia's hand and led her to the kitchen.

"I guess we can let ourselves in," Celinda gritted her teeth with annoyance.

"Make sure you lock the door!" Ms. Ellis called out, wishing she could've left both Celinda and her sister outside. "Baby, you ready for your surprise?" she asked Amelia who was holding her hand tightly.

"Yes!" she smiled widely. "Daddy!" Amelia screamed running into her father's arms.

"My beautiful baby girl!" Prevan lifted his daughter up in the air and held her tightly in his arms. It took all his strength not to breakdown in tears. He hadn't seen his daughter in months and holding her again made Prevan weak.

"You came through with that surprise," Caleb said to his mother when they walked out the kitchen, so father and daughter could have some alone time together.

"The joy I saw in both of their eyes will forever stay with me." Ms. Ellis was beyond ecstatic. Her overwhelming bliss quickly came to a halt when she saw Celinda sitting in the living room next to her sister.

"I know Amelia is thrilled to see her dad," Celinda's sister, Mia, said smiling.

"Yes, she is," Ms. Ellis snapped. "You all don't have to wait here. You can come back later and get Amelia or Caleb can drop her off."

"We prefer to stay here and wait," Celinda countered.

"I don't..."

"Chill ma." Caleb cut his mother off and said. "Let them stay. It's Prevan's first day home, we don't want no drama."

Ms. Ellis nodded her head in agreement. Tossing Amelia's mother and aunt out her house would only give Celinda another reason to play victim she reasoned.

"It's the least you can do after I rushed over here with no notice. I didn't have to bring Amelia over here," Celinda popped.

"I said you could stay. I ain't said nothin' 'bout you runnin' yo' mouth to my mom," Caleb popped back before his mother used Celinda's smart comment as a reason to curse her out.

Celinda rolled her eyes, sitting back in the chair with an attitude. Mia began fidgeting her fingers, looking uncomfortable as if she preferred not to be there. The tension in the room was almost unbearable for everyone but that didn't stop Mia from acknowledging her crush.

"It's good to see you again, Caleb." Mia spoke so softly you could barely hear her. Caleb didn't respond, so this time Mia made sure to add some depth to her voice. "It's good to see you again, Caleb."

"Cool," Caleb said giving a one word response. On the real, he thought Mia seemed like a decent chick. She might've even been a sweet girl but Caleb gave her little to no play based on who her scandalous ass sister. She was guilty by association which voided her out in Caleb's mind.

"Mommy look, Daddy finally came back home!" Amelia belted when she came out the kitchen, sitting on her father's shoulders.

"I see." Celinda stood up and went over to both of them. She wrapped her arms around Prevan. "I'm happy you're home." He appeared less than enthusiastic to see his baby mother but kept his emotions in check around their daughter.

"Damn, I pray your brother learned his lesson and don't fall for her bullshit again," Ms. Ellis whispered to her son.

Caleb prayed for that too, especially since he had to sell his soul to the devil to make this miracle happen. Initially Caleb wasn't even convinced Arnez would deliver on his promise. Once he hired a top notch attorney, he was able to secure a bail hearing for his brother. The prosecutor on the case, let it be known she would make an argument before the presiding judge that bail be denied but it never happened. A few days before the hearing, the prosecutor's star witness was found dead in what appeared to be a drug deal gone bad. With the so-called victim and only witness in the case unable to testify, the case died with him. The prosecutor had no choice but to drop the charges and soon after Prevan was released from jail. Arnez didn't give Caleb any details how everything went down because he wanted him to be sincerely clueless when the cops came asking questions which they did.

Caleb was so worried his brother's nightmare wouldn't be ending anytime soon, he didn't even tell his mother that Prevan might be getting released until he got the call directly from his brother that he'd been released. So, although Caleb had no love for Arnez, he was grateful he orchestrated the right scheme to get Prevan home. Now he wondered what it would cost him because he knew Arnez would be coming to collect and Caleb better be ready to pay up.

Chapter Thirteen

Give Me The Reason

"T-Roc, I was glad you called," Renny said taking a seat.

"I'm glad you were able to meet with me on such short notice. I hope I didn't make you go too far out the way coming to Century City. This is one of my favorite restaurants and living in New York, I rarely get to come here anymore," T-Roc explained. "They are one of the only spots that serve an extremely rare Caspian Sea beluga caviar," he smiled taking a sip of some 1981 Krug.

"You get no complaints from me. It's one of the reasons we always got along, we both have great taste." The two men laughed.

"How's Nichelle doing and your son?"

"Both are doing very well. We're actually heading to your neck of the woods in a couple weeks."

"Let me guess, the get together for Genesis's daughter Genevieve."

"No doubt. Nichelle is excited about seeing her only niece who was named after her. She has baby fever. God willing we'll be expecting one of our own very soon."

"It'll happen for you. Nichelle is a sweetheart who will make an incredible mother," T-Roc stated.

"She's been an incredible mother to Elijah. He adores her as do I. But I know you didn't request this emergency dinner for me to go on about how much I love my wife. What can I do for you, T-Roc?"

"First, I need you to promise anonymity on this," T-Roc stated.

"I give you my word," Renny assured him.

"Good. What do you know about a woman named Astrid Bryant? With the way, your eyes just shifted when I mentioned her name, it must be a lot."

"What made you ask me about Astrid?"

"Because she's married to Delondo. I also remember he introduced her when we were in Philly. I was cool with Delondo but the two of you were very close."

"We were tight at one time but..."

"Renny, don't lie to me. This is some serious shit. A couple of years ago my daughter received treatment at a center in CA."

"Is that the reason you came out this way?"

"Yes, it is. I went to the facility to get some information. While going over the visitation list, Astrid came to see my daughter multiple times. On one visitation both Astrid and Maya came together. Justina was very unstable and vulnerable during that period of time. I believe those women took advantage of my daughter's condition but I can't figure out why they would be working together. Renny, if you know what the link is, you need to tell me."

"Astrid is Arnez's sister."

"What! Arnez tried to kill Delondo, why would he marry his sister?" T-Roc was taken aback as he wasn't expecting that answer.

"Delondo doesn't know."

"Why the hell not! Don't you think that's something he needs to know?"

"Listen, I was concerned too." Renny lowered the base in his voice trying not to draw attention from the other patrons in the restaurant but his words were stern. "I went to see her the day after we ran into them. I was prepared to tell Delondo but Astrid swore when they got together, she had no clue of his history with Arnez and they were already married by the time she had contact with him again. Astrid said she lost contact with her brother and eventually found out Arnez was dead."

"You believed her story?"

"If I hadn't then I would've gone straight to Delondo. They have a daughter together. I didn't want to risk fuckin' up his family if Astrid was telling me the truth."

"Do you still believe her story now?" T-Roc leaned forward and asked with cynicism.

Renny fell back in his chair as if defeated. You could see the fury in his face. "Nah I don't. Astrid lied to me. If she was in cahoots with Maya then she had to be dealing with Arnez."

"When Genesis found Talisa, the man who was holding her hostage got killed, before they were able to find out who he was working for. Do you think it could be Astrid?"

"That's a bit farfetched. I mean Astrid was always a schemer but she's not smart enough to pull something of that magnitude off. Arnez was probably pulling the strings behind the scenes and Astrid did what she was told. Since Arnez and Maya are both dead, it's probably why it's been quiet because Astrid has gone back to being just a dope man's wife."

"Maybe you're right but even though Arnez is dead, you still need to tell Delondo about Astrid. He might be married to the enemy and not even know it."

"That's one conversation I'm not looking forward to having, but you're right. Delondo deserves to know the truth especially if Astrid could potentially bring him down."

"She gets more and more beautiful every time I see her," Precious gushed holding Genevieve. "She is the sweetest little thing.

"I know. I can't believe how blessed I am. It's like night and day from when I had my son," Skylar said.

"Your son is such a sweetheart, was he a

difficult baby?"

"No, not at all. I mean I was struggling so much back then. His father wasn't around to help financially and I barely had two dimes to rub together. It was stressful. But with Genevieve, I don't have a care in the world. Genesis makes sure our needs are overly met."

"I don't think anyone would deny Genesis is a good guy. I'm sure he also feels guilty he can't be with his daughter on a daily basis like he'd want."

"Oh, so now you're saying it's guilt money?" Skylar snapped.

"Don't get defensive," Precious scoffed. "All I'm saying is, Genesis probably tries to overcompensate because he'd never want Genevieve or even you for that matter, to think you're not important to him because he has another family. We both know Genesis is very thoughtful and considerate of other people's feelings."

"Very true."

"Genesis is generous but stop trying to act like guilt isn't one of the reasons he's throwing all sorts of extra money your way. Or maybe you do know but it's easier for you to take advantage if you pretend you don't."

Skylar wanted to pretend she didn't hear what Precious said but that was difficult to do with her standing in her face. "Fine! Maybe I am slightly taking advantage of the fact Genesis feels guilty," she confessed. "I mean we were supposed to be a family...remember."

"Yes, I remember and so does Genesis. And you all are family but he does have a wife. A wife who is putting together a very nice soiree for little Genevieve," Precious smiled, gently squeezing her Goddaughter's cheek.

"I still can't believe I agreed to that although Talisa didn't leave me much of a choice," Skylar complained.

"That's what you get for being all up in Oscar De La Renta spending her husband's money," Precious mocked.

"Why can't Talisa be like most wives and want nothing to do with her husband's ex."

"Because Talisa is playing to win and by you agreeing to this party, I guess you are too."

"I can't get nothing past you, can I, Precious?" Skylar smirked.

"I know all the tricks. I invented half of them and the other half, I've dabbled in. So, take heed to my suggestion. Don't overly play your hand, Skylar. I've seen shit go to shambles overnight. You don't want that to happen to you," Precious warned.

Genesis walked up behind Talisa who was doing her hair in the hallway mirror leading to the master bathroom. "You look beautiful," he said before sprinkling kisses on the side of her neck. He then took his hands and released the sash on her silk robe and let it fall to the floor.

"I have to get ready for an appointment I have," Talisa said between moans while her husband's hands danced across every curve of her naked body.

"I know but let me feel inside of you for just a second," he whispered in her ear, using the tip of his finger to caress her hardened nipples.

"Only for a second," she said breathlessly. Genesis had already slid inside his wife before Talisa got her last word out. He had her pinned forward on the Carrara marble topped vanity, taking control and moving with precision. She stared up at the clear Venetian chandelier as each stroke sent her deeper into a daze. Those seconds turned to minutes and minutes into an hour.

"You also do this to me," Talisa turned to Genesis and said, after their love making went from the vanity to the bed.

"I can't help myself. You're my ultimate addiction." Genesis leaned over to kiss Talisa.

"No, no, no," she teased, waving her finger. "This is about to lead to round two and I'm already running late due to round one."

"Then promise me we can continue this tonight."

"As sexy as you look lying in bed, I can easily make and keep that promise."

"Sexy...I thought you were the sexy one," Genesis gave a sly grin.

"Thank your personal trainer. He has your body super cut. Is that the correct lingo?" Talisa joked. "Seriously, your muscle definition is perfect. Now, I have to get in the shower." She blew Genesis a kiss and hurried off.

Genesis was about to get out of bed and join his wife in the shower when he saw Supreme was calling him. "Supreme, what's going on?"

"Same shit, different day."

"Are you calling to RSVP?"

"No." Supreme and Genesis chuckled.

"You do know that was supposed to be a joke," Genesis continued to laugh.

"Man, I get yo' sense of humor. But you already know Precious and I will be there."

"She is the Godmother."

"Exactly and she takes the title seriously. How does it feel being a father again to a little baby after all these years?"

"Amazing. I even stepped up my workout regimen. I wanna be in top notch shape, so when she starts running around the park, going swimming, or playing sports, I can keep up with her."

"I'm happy for you, Genesis. You have your wife back and now a beautiful baby girl. Your life is good."

"It really is. I wake up every morning with a smile on my face."

"I'm glad to hear that."

"We got to talking about everything else, I never gave you a chance to tell me why you called," Genesis said.

"On the real, I was just checking up on you. You were on my mind. I'm glad to hear you're in a good place."

"Thanks, Supreme. You're a major part of the reason my life is this perfect. I'll forever be grateful to you for that."

"It's all love, Genesis. I'll see you soon."

When Supreme got off the phone with Genesis, he regretted not coming clean with him about the real reason he called. But he'd never heard the man he now considered to be a very good friend sound so content. His voice was up-beat and positive. Genesis really did seem to be in the perfect place in his life. It was the only reason Supreme stopped himself from telling him there was a chance Arnez might still be alive. Instead, he decided to wait until his private investigator gathered all the information and he could go to him with facts. Supreme didn't want to disrupt Genesis's idyllic life, turning it upside down, if in fact Arnez was truly a dead man.

Chapter Fourteen

Deadweight

"Seventeen I was charging niggas seventeen!" Caleb rapped the line while listening to the Rick Ross track War Ready in his brand new whip. This was the first time he had taken the fully loaded spectral blue chromalflair, satin matte finish Range Rover Autobiography with 22" 6 spoke diamond turned finish wheels out on the street, since leaving the dealership.

"Nigga, this shit is nice!" Floyd, Caleb's right-hand man hollered when he hopped in the passenger side. Floyd bit down on his fist. "I see why you keep this joint locked up. It look a little bigger than some of the other ones I seen."

"Yeah, I got the long wheelbase version. It got like an additional rear legroom of 7.3 inches. I'ma tall dude, so you know," Caleb cracked.

"I'm in love. I'll take this over some pussy any day," Floyd cackled.

"Nigga, you crazy. I figured since we going to what supposed to be some upscale club party, I could pull out my official shit."

"Ain't nobody there gon' have this shit. A nigga can pull up in a Lambo but yo' shit is swagged the fuck out. But you deserve it." Floyd nodded giving Caleb some dap.

"Thanks man," Caleb said smiling, which he rarely did. But he knew Floyd meant that shit. Floyd had done every petty crime he pulled since they were twelve years old. When he started working for Khyree, Caleb wasn't able to bring him in the fold but he always looked out for his friend. Now that he was the man, he wanted Floyd right by his side. Unlike Caleb who many would mistake for a pro NBA player, due to his six-four height and well-built body frame, Floyd on the other hand was five-six but he had the heart of giant. Not only that, he was loyal and Caleb valued loyalty more than any other attribute.

"Where's Prevan? The birthday boy ain't riding wit' us?"

"Nope. He decided to roll wit' Celinda," Caleb huffed.

"He back wit' his baby mom? Ain't no way!" Floyd shook his head.

"Yep."

"I don't care what nobody says, I know his baby mom set his ass up. She call Prevan all hysterical sayin' some dude hit her. He get there but she gon' and two niggas try to rob him. Prevan shoot one of the dudes, the other get ghost. After he arrested, Celinda claim that ain't the guy that hit her." Floyd paused giving Caleb the 'what tha fuck' face.

"Man, I'm wit' you," Caleb nodded

"Then dude flip it and says it was Prevan who tried to rob him. Since Celinda claim he ain't the dude who hit her, there ain't no other witnesses and he the one wit' the bullet, Prevan get hit wit' an attempted murder charge. Now explain that bullshit to me?!"

"Ain't no explaining it. That broad shiesty."

"You know I heard Celinda was fuckin' wit' the other nigga who got ghost," Floyd added.

"I heard that shit too. I even brought it up to Prevan but he wasn't tryna hear it so I let it go."

"Homegirl Hispanic. I heard a lot them be into that spirit work...you know to get they men under their control."

"You don't believe in that bullshit," Caleb laughed.

"It must be something. Why else would Prevan keep fuckin' wit' her. Pussy can't make a nigga that dumb," Floyd frowned.

"Honestly, I think my brother determined to have this happy little family wit' him, Celinda, and Amelia. The shit done made him turn a blind eye to how trifling his baby mama is."

"Prevan better get his mind right. You worked a miracle so them charges was dropped. Next time his baby mama might do him in and he won't be so lucky."

"If Celinda fuck my brother over again, won't none of this shit matter, 'cause that broad will have to deal wit' me. Now let's go have some fun," Caleb said pulling up in front of the club.

Astrid was walking out the kitchen when she heard the sound of a cell phone vibrating. "Delondo must've left his phone when he ran outside to get Delilah," she remarked, going over to see who was calling her husband. When Astrid saw Renny's name across the screen, a feeling of uneasiness immediately kicked in. She was tempted to answer the call but decided to see if he left a text message or even left a voicemail. Astrid had cracked her husband's passcode a long time ago when she suspected he was cheating. Periodically she would listen to his messages to make sure he wasn't fuckin' around.

D I'll be in town next week and I need to see you. It's about Astrid.

"That sonofabitch!" Astrid fumed when she read the text.

"Don't forget you promised me ice cream, daddy." Astrid heard her daughter saying as they were coming back inside the house.

"I know. Let me get my car keys and we're leaving," Delondo said. Astrid quickly deleted Renny's text, snuck out the kitchen and hurried upstairs before Delondo and Delilah could see her.

"Fuck!" she mumbled under her breath as anxiety began to take over.

"Astrid, I'm taking Delilah to get ice cream!" Delondo hollered out.

"Okay! Make sure you bring me some back!" she yelled, happy they were leaving so she could call her brother. Once they were gone she got on the phone.

"Let me call you back." Arnez told Astrid the moment he answered her call.

"I need to talk to you now. It's important!"

"It will have to wait. I'm dealing with something right now."

"I can't..." Before Astrid could finish her sentence, she realized her brother had hung up on her. Unwilling to wait, she grabbed her purse and car keys and headed straight to Arnez's place.

"Here, I brought you over some champagne," Mia smiled.

"I'm straight." Caleb put his hand up, pushing the glass away.

"You look really nice tonight. I mean you always look good but I've never seen you dressed up before," she said nervously staring at his attire. Caleb was draped in head to toe Balmain. He had a black single button shawl blazer with a silk lapel collar, welt pocket at chest, flap pockets at the waist with a logo engraved gold tone hardware. Keeping it dressy yet casual cool, he paired it with a crewneck, rib knit wool blend jersey t-shirt in white, some distressed black denim jeans, ribbed panel at the knees with contrast stitching in tan, and of course some ice links for the wrist.

"Thanks," he politely said.

"That's it? You're not going to say I look nice too?" Mia asked.

"No, but I will if it'll make you go away."

"You don't have to be so mean. I've been nothing but nice to you. Why don't you like me?"

"I guess you guilty by association. Yo' sister ain't shit, so I'm assuming it's hereditary."

"So, what, I ain't shit neither. I love my sister but I'm nothing like Celinda."

"Mia, what do you want from me? You seem like an okay girl but yo' sister has left a very bad taste in my mouth. If you think I can get past that and date you, it ain't gon' happen. Stop wasting yo' time." The sharpness of Caleb's words cut Mia like a knife.

"How can you be so young but so cold." Mia's voice was shaky. When Caleb glanced up and saw the pain on her face and tears in her eyes, for a moment he felt bad but he quickly shook it off.

"How 'bout you ask yo' sister that question."

Mia had no response so she walked away in defeat.

"That girl been sniffing behind you forever. You need to go 'head and give her tha dick," Floyd joked.

"Shit, I'm tryna get rid of her," Caleb shrugged. "If only I could get my brother to get rid of Celinda." He watched in disgust as the two of them were glued together in the VIP section. Caleb loved his big brother and made him a high ranking member of his team. Prevan was making real money now and sharing the wealth with a woman who almost cost him his life which showed weakness and poor judgment. For both of their sake, Caleb hoped he didn't end up regretting bringing his brother into the fold.

Chapter Fifteen

Small World

"Fatima, where's my brother?" Astrid asked the woman who took care of Arnez, when she answered the door.

"He's outside on the terrace. Mrs. Bryant, he has company!" she called out.

Astrid had already brushed past his caretaker and was damn near running through the condo while the woman was still talking. She swung opened the glass French doors and there was

Arnez with a man she'd never seen before.

"I told you I would call you back," Arnez said, glancing over at his sister, annoyed she took it upon herself to just show up.

"And I told you this couldn't wait!" Astrid shot back.

"We're done for now but keep me updated," Arnez stated, then dismissed the man. He went right by Astrid in a robotic way, without speaking a word.

"Who was that?" Astrid was curious to know.

"Don't worry about it. I'm more concerned what was so important you disregarded my request and came storming through here in a panic."

"My life is going to shambles!" Astrid threw her hands up, pacing back and forth. "How can this be happening!?"

"How can what be happening? Will you please stop being fuckin' dramatic and tell me what the hell is going on!" Arnez barked.

"Renny sent a text to Delondo today."

"A text saying what?"

"He'll be in town next week and wanted to see Delondo"

"Okay. So, what," Arnez shrugged.

"He said it was about me. Renny is going to

tell Delondo I'm your sister and probably a lot more than that. What am I gonna do?!" Astrid cried. "Delondo can't find out about my past, he'll leave me."

"What did you tell Delondo after he asked you about the text from Renny?"

"He didn't see the text. I deleted it before he had a chance to read it," Astrid explained.

"Very good. That buys us some time."

"Not much! My life will be ruined!" Astrid was becoming hysterical.

"Can you keep your voice down. Fatima and the entire fuckin' street can probably hear you."

Astrid was nervously fidgeting with the leather skinny bow belt wrapped around her dress. She noticed a glass of liquor sitting on a table near Arnez. Without asking, she reached for the glass and gulped it down. The strong alcohol burned her throat going down but that didn't stop Astrid from searching for more. She wanted to numb her anxiety and one drink wouldn't be enough.

"Arnez, tell me what to do. You always have the answers. You have to help me," she pleaded.

Such a feeble woman you are, Arnez thought to himself. But he still had use for his sister so, he played it carefully.

"Come sit down." He patted the chair next to him. Her movements were insanely slow it seemed she was walking in slow motion which made Arnez even more incensed. He maintained his cool, seeing his sister was on the verge of having a breakdown.

"I can't lose my husband," Astrid said between sobs.

"You may not have a choice."

"Don't say that, Arnez. There's always a way. Isn't that your motto. Look how long you were able to keep Genesis and Talisa apart."

"This situation is different."

"Maybe if I beg Renny to keep his mouth shut he will," Astrid reasoned.

"You and I both know how Renny feels about you. Obviously, he somehow found out the story you told him was a lie. Now he's going to tell Delondo everything he knows about you which he probably wanted to anyway. You only have two choices, Astrid."

"Which are?"

"Take Delilah and leave, or kill Delondo," Arnez casually suggested.

"Kill my husband!" Astrid jumped up. "You want me to kill the father of my child?!"

"What I know is Renny can't speak to Delondo because if he does, all of my plans will be ruined."

"Not necessarily."

"Oh please." Arnez flipped his hand at his sister. "You'll breakdown and confess it all once Delondo starts grilling you. I can't allow that to happen, especially now."

"Is something else going on?" Astrid asked.

"The man who left when you got here is my eyes on the streets. Word has it, Supreme has someone asking around about me," Arnez revealed.

"What! Supreme left you for dead. Why would he think you're alive?"

"My guy is still gathering information but supposedly it's some female putting this rumor out there."

"A female...the only females that know you're alive is Fatima and me. There has to be more to this."

"It could be some bullshit gossip but whoever and wherever it's coming from, has gotten Supreme's attention which I don't need. He has the best men on his payroll. Hell, he found the fuckin' island I had Talisa on for all those years," Arnez scoffed. "That's why this Renny and Delondo meeting can never happen. If this ain't six degrees of separation. Them niggas get to talking, putting the pieces together, it's a wrap for me."

"Arnez, I won't let that happen. You're my brother. You always came through for me when nobody else did." Astrid knelt down by Arnez and laid her head down on his upper leg. "If I have to choose between you and Delondo, I choose you."

"I knew you wouldn't let me down." Arnez said stroking Astrid's hair, with his signature devilish smile spread across his face.

"If you keep bringing in all this loot, I may have to expand you out of Philly maybe let you oversee Philly too," Amir said to Caleb as they exchanged money.

"Man, I'm down. There's twenty-four hours in a day. All I need is three to sleep and can work the rest."

"I respect your grind but you young. Go out and enjoy some of this money you making and I don't mean just buying a nice ass ride that you rarely drive," Amir cracked. "You ain't got no girl?"

"Hell no! Girls complicate shit. I'm focused on stackin' paper. Women will always be readily available especially when you chipped the fuck up."

"You got a lot of fuckin' sense to be seventeen."

"When you come from my hood and seen what I seen, you betta have some sense or you'll be fucked up out here," Caleb shrugged.

"I want you to go someplace with me."

"When, now? I thought you said you had to turn right around and head back to New York."

"Not today, next week," Amir clarified.

"What's going on next week?"

"My dad recently had a little girl and he's having a get together to celebrate. It's a low key family and friends type thing."

"And you want me to come?"

"Yeah, why you look so surprised. You part of the family now and I think it's time you met everyone but especially my father," Amir told him.

"I'ma meet the Genesis Taylor?" Caleb shook his head. "Not sure I'm ready for that."

"Trust me you ready. He's been impressed with how you dominating here in Philly, we all are."

"Yo I'm honored."

"Does that mean you're accepting my invite?"

"How I'ma say no to celebrating wit' Genesis

Taylor?! Of course, I accept!"

"Cool." Amir and Caleb gave each other a pound as Amir was leaving. "I'll see you next week then, but we'll talk before that, like we always do."

"No doubt."

Amir and Caleb would be talking before that, if not every day, then every other day. The two had become close. Caleb was like the little brother Amir never had and Amir was like the big brother Caleb always wanted. There was a mutual respect, to the point that Caleb had begun keeping his distance from Arnez. He wanted no part of bringing down Genesis or anyone close to him but Caleb knew he was in too deep. He would have to start feeding Arnez information before he became suspicious. Now all Caleb had to figure out is what that information should be.

Chapter Sixteen

Limited Options

Justina was lounging by the pool, sipping champagne and listening to Rihanna's 'Needed Me', she tilted her sunglasses up when she noticed a familiar number calling. Her finger went to hit the decline button but opted for accept instead.

"Why are you calling me?" Justina snapped when she answered.

"Because I need your help."

Hearing the word 'need' made Justina quickly turn off the Rihanna song as if listening to it had somehow jinxed her and made her receive this call.

"Astrid, we agreed no further communication. There is nothing I can help you with."

"Please don't hang up!" she shouted. "I'm leaving Philly and taking Delilah with me."

"Leaving Philly. What about your husband?"

"It's complicated but I have to get out of town fast. I know you're in Miami and Delondo wouldn't think to look for me there."

"You want to come stay with me? That's not gonna work." Justina dismissed the idea without hesitation.

"Why not? Nobody there knows who I am."

"And I want to keep it like that. If Aaliyah or Amir come over and see you they're gonna start asking me a ton of questions. If they find out you're Arnez's sister, all hell is gonna break loose." Justina fumed.

"How would they find out? My own husband doesn't even know. Please, Justina. With Maya and Arnez both dead, I have no one else to turn to but you."

"How long do you need to stay?"

"A few weeks most. I'm getting housing set up and new identities for me and Delilah but I can't wait here while it's being done. I promise to keep a really low profile. Please, Justina," Astrid begged.

"Fine. Maybe I can tell anyone who might ask you're related to me on my mother's side of the family, since hardly anybody including me has met them." Justina rolled her eyes wondering why she never changed her number.

"Justina, thank you so much. I'll book our flights tonight and I'll let you know what day we're coming. It'll probably be by the end of the week. I'll call you back and confirm everything once I know for sure."

"Okay," Justina said hanging up. She put her sunglasses back down to cover her eyes but that did nothing to hide her frustration. Astrid and her daughter hadn't even arrived yet and Justina felt like she was suffering from an anxiety attack. She was trying to forget the alliance she once shared with Maya, Astrid, and although she never met him, Arnez too. Now, in less than a week, a huge reminder of her shady past would be living with her. For Astrid's sake, Justina hoped her stay would be short lived.

"This is exactly what I need," Genesis commented to Amir after finishing an intense workout with their personal trainer and now they were relaxing in the steam room.

"Yep, I needed this too. Spending all that time in Philly got me slacking on working out," Amir moaned closing his eyes and taking in the heat. "I'm back on track now though."

"Yeah, being on the grind will do that. I remember when I was your age, I would be hittin' the streets so hard, sometimes I would go days with hardly any sleep. All I wanted to do was make money."

"You sound like that dude, Caleb. He grind so hard, he make me feel like I'm slippin'," Amir conceded.

"His turnaround rate and profit is impressive. I used to think it was Khyree working hard, now I see it was actually one of his soldiers. You called it right, letting Caleb take over. You continue making those type of executive decisions, I might be able to retire from the business sooner than I thought."

"Thanks for trusting me on this, especially since it wasn't the popular decision. Lorenzo and Nico both wanted to veto it."

"They were concerned with his age and figured he lacked the necessary experience to handle the volume for a city like Philly. Caleb proved them wrong and me too for that matter."

"Dad, you never mentioned you were concerned."

"What's the point of me handing more responsibility over to you if I don't let you trust your own instincts. A big part of not only surviving in this drug game but also be successful, is following your instincts. I didn't want my apprehensions make you second guess yourself, so I remained silent. Glad I did," Genesis nodded.

"Me too. Hope you don't mind but I invited Caleb to the baby celebration that mom is putting together."

"I didn't realize you and Caleb had become so close."

"I'll admit, I've taken a liking to him. I guess him saving my life might've played a slight role," Amir said smiling. "He's like the younger brother I never had."

"I can see that. No matter how diligent this Caleb guy is, he's still a seventeen-year-old kid. He needs guidance like any other teenager. Don't forget it," Genesis cautioned.

"Point taken."

"Good. Now that we're done talking about

the little brother you never had, let's talk about the sister you do have. Why haven't you gone to see Genevieve?"

"Work, all my trips to Philly, hasn't left me any time," Amir said.

"You make time for family."

But do you even really know if Genevieve is our family? You're so willing to take the word of Skylar without any proof. You say she's my little sister but until I know for sure, I'm not ready to embrace Genevieve, Amir thought to himself but didn't have the nerves to say to his father.

"You're right. I guess I'm still getting used to the idea of having a little sister."

"She's not going anywhere, so you better get used to it. If your mother is okay with it, then you shouldn't have any problems either."

"You truly believe mom is okay with it?"

"Of course, she is. Your mother wouldn't have volunteered to do this get together if she wasn't okay with it. Talisa has been to Skylar's place a few times to see Genevieve."

"She's doing that because she loves you not because she's okay," Amir refuted.

"Has your mother said something to you? If so, then speak up."

Amir could hear his father becoming defensive. Suggesting he get a DNA test was out of the question now.

"No, she hasn't said anything. I'm concerned about her that's all. She's already been through so much." Amir put his head down. You could see he was torn.

"She's your mother, you want to protect her. You're being a good son." Genesis put his hand on Amir's shoulder. "I apologize if I came off as hostile. I adore Genevieve and I want us all to be a family."

"Don't worry about it, dad. It'll all work out," Amir said, looking up at his father.

"Are you positive this is what you want? To leave Philly and create a new identity for you and Delilah?" Arnez asked Astrid.

"I don't have a choice. It's either leave or admit the truth to Delondo which we both know is out of the question."

"What will you tell Delilah? She'll want to know why she's no longer able to see her father. It would be much easier for you tell her he's dead."

Astrid cut her eyes at Arnez and walked towards the massive window, staring out at the view of the Delaware River. Leaving her husband was a devastating blow and her feelings for him ran deeper than she even knew.

"Killing my husband is not an option, Arnez."

"I didn't say you had to kill him. I would handle everything for you. I'm not that cruel, Astrid."

"So, you having him killed would somehow lessen the blow?" she turned to her brother and asked. "He shouldn't lose his life because we fell in love."

"Oh, you're in love with him." Arnez twiddled his thumbs together pondering what his sister said. "This is news to me. "I thought you simply had been looking for a man to take care of you and Delondo was your best option. You know, so you wouldn't have to spend your life struggling like our mother did. When did falling in love become part of the equation?"

"I'll wait for you to make all the arrangements for where Delilah and I will be living, until then we'll be staying with Justina." Astrid stated not responding to Arnez's question.

"I'm still surprised Justina agreed to let you come but I'm sure you made her feel obligated to do so. You didn't..."

"No, I didn't." Astrid cut Arnez off, already

knowing what he was about to ask. "Justina believes you are dead like everyone else."

"Not everyone. Supreme isn't giving up. I hate I made an enemy of him. With his resources, he was always very useful. Now..." Arnez's voice faded off.

"Just continue to keep a low profile and don't have Caleb or anyone else make any moves that might possibly bring unwanted attention to you. The rumors will die down and Supreme will move on."

Arnez heard what Astrid said but he knew it wasn't that simple. His sister lived in a world of simple thoughts and ideas, she always did. It was one of the reasons she was easy for him to manipulate. Supreme on the other hand came from the same world he did, where complicated was the norm. If a rumor had been ignited to the point Supreme was investigating, he wouldn't give up until he had concrete evidence Arnez was either dead or alive.

Chapter Seventeen

Party Confessions

"Talisa, did an incredible job putting this together," Precious gushed to Skylar.

"She did hire an event planner. It's not like she did it all on her own," Skylar remarked.

"Someone sounds a little pissy," Precious smirked, sipping her champagne. "I thought you would be impressed with how lovely everything is. I mean look at this place. She transformed your beautiful penthouse apartment into something out of a fairy tale book."

Skylar hated to admit it but the place was decorated beautifully. There was lace linen with a blush pink underlay and blush/violet glassware filled with orchids to compliment the overall color scheme. There was a unique array of pastel tones for the centerpieces. A hanging rose treatment was created for the backdrop of the cake table with Genevieve's name placed in the center. There was also a long candle wall with lush tall showpieces, highlighting memorable images of Genevieve alone, with Genesis, and with Skylar.

"Can I get a picture of you and the baby standing over there?" the photographer came over and asked Skylar.

"I'll be happy to!" Skylar beamed ready to get away from Precious especially since she saw Talisa making a beeline towards them.

"Where is Skylar running off to? I wanted to see if she was ready for everyone to sit down and eat." Talisa asked Precious.

"The photographer wanted her to take some pictures with Genevieve," Precious smiled. "Congratulations on putting together such an amazing get together. I don't think my bridal shower was this nice," Precious teased.

"Thank you. I wanted it to be special."

"I'm sure you did. Your point has been made."

"I don't follow you." Talisa seemed confused.

"Surely this breathtaking soiree wasn't for our benefit. You wanted Skylar to know you were in this for the long haul and you delivered the message in such a classy way, I might add. Very impressive. Me on the other hand, would've just kicked her ass."

Talisa almost choked on the hors d'oeuvre she was eating. "Excuse me," she laughed. "I wasn't expecting you to say that."

"I think your way is much more productive. I mean violence leads to more violence. I've never had a problem with that but it's definitely not for everyone."

"Well, thank you, Precious. I'm thinking it's a compliment."

"Yes! Mos def a compliment. You're handling this entire situation with a lot of grace. I know it can't be easy."

"Is it that obvious?" Talisa wanted to know.

"Not at all. You're flawless but I'm a woman, so I get it. In time, it will become easier."

"You really think so, because I'm not so sure."

"I'm positive."

"How can you be so confident about that?" Talisa wondered.

"Because Genesis has been in love with you

from the first time I met him years ago and that's even when he believed he would never see your face again. The man simply adores you."

"Thank you for saying that," Talisa blushed.

"We all need to be reminded of the truth sometimes, even when we already know what it is," Precious said warmly.

"Thanks again, Precious. My son just walked in. We'll catch up later." Talisa blew her a kiss and hurried off.

"That seemed very cozy," Chantal giggled sneaking up on Precious. "How are you able to juggle being the Godmother and close friend to Genesis's baby mama and be friendly with the wife? Do tell."

"There's nothing to tell. I keep it real with all parties involved," Precious popped.

"Just be prepared when one of them asks you to pick a side. We both know it's gonna happen sooner or later."

"I got this covered."

"I know. Honestly, I didn't come over here to antagonize you," Chantal said, which made Precious look at her suspiciously.

"What other reason would make you be in my space?"

"In the past, I would've come over and

made some catty comment that there are only a handful of men here and you've slept with at least three of them but I want us to move beyond that," Chantal said unable to resist one last jab. Precious was about to drag Chantal for filth but before she could, her adversary said, "I actually came over to apologize."

"Excuse me?!"

"I put you and your daughter through so much. I'm embarrassed and ashamed of my actions in the past. I hurt my family and humiliated myself with such reckless behavior. I know you'll never forget what I've done but hopefully one day you will forgive me."

"Has your doctor put you on some new medication, Chantal?" Precious gave her the side eye, like 'who the fuck is this woman standing next to me?' "In case you're wondering, that wasn't a trick question or a joke."

"Listen, I get it. I really do. Whatever you think of me, I deserve it. I've done horrible things. Luckily, Aaliyah was able to move past what I did and not hold it against Justina. They're now best friends again. Maybe one day, things will be cordial between us. I won't take up anymore of your time. And by the way, lilac is truly your color. That dress is beautiful on you and your skin is glowing," Chantal gave one last compliment before walking off.

"What in the hell is that crazy bitch up to?" Precious mumbled under her breath, knowing whatever it was, it couldn't be good.

Caleb got caught up with some work at the last minute, so he was late leaving Philly. Amir told him to come through once he got to the city. Now that he pulled up in front of the high rise luxury building in the heart of Manhattan, a feeling he wasn't used to came over him...nervousness. He thought maybe it was because he didn't know anyone who would be there besides Amir, or maybe it wasn't nervousness he was feeling but instead, guilt. He had been invited to a family celebration but was working with the man who wanted to take down the patriarch of that family. Initially, Caleb was able to push that in the back of his mind and leave it there, now not so much. He was betraying the man he had nothing but love for.

This how rich people living, Caleb said to himself when he walked into Skylar's penthouse apartment. *He got his baby mother living like this,*

I can only imagine how Genesis's living. Damn!

"You made it!" Amir greeted Caleb enthusiastically when he saw him come in. "I was worried for a minute."

"I told you I was coming. Here I brought a gift for your little sister." Caleb handed Amir the professionally wrapped present.

"You didn't have to do this. You making me look bad. I didn't even get her a gift," Amir joked but was serious. "Follow me, I want you to meet my mom and dad."

Caleb was taking everything in as he followed behind Amir. *Is that Supreme and T-Roc standing over there*, he thought amazed seeing the music industry legends in the building. Caleb was a bit overwhelmed. Being around all this greatness had opened his eyes to a whole other world and he soaked it in. This was the life he wanted for himself.

"Mom, dad, I want you to meet my good friend, Caleb."

"It's a pleasure to meet you," Talisa beamed.

"Yes, it is. Amir, has spoken highly of you." Genesis reached out and shook Caleb's hand.

"Thank you, sir. It's an honor to finally meet you. Where I'm from, you're a legend."

"I have a lot of love for the great city of

Philadelphia. Next time Amir goes, I'll have to accompany him and let you show us around. I'm sure a lot has stayed the same but it's also changed."

"For sure," Caleb nodded with a wide grin. "The streets would lose their mind if they saw me with the great Genesis Taylor."

"I want you to meet one of my other partners, Nico Carter," Genesis said putting his arm around Caleb. "We'll be right back."

"I see your father has taken a liking to your friend," Talisa commented as the two of them strolled off.

"I knew he would. Caleb reminds me a lot of dad."

"That doesn't bother you, does it?"

"I know when dad sees someone like Caleb, he can relate to him because they both started from the bottom, had to struggle. That's not my story. Honestly, everyone knows I was handed this life."

"Son, don't ever feel bad because you were born into money. When much is given, much is required. As long as you don't take that for granted, you'll be fine."

While his mother was speaking to him, Amir noticed something or someone had caught her attention. He turned in the direction she was staring at and saw his dad holding Genevieve while smiling at Skylar.

"It would be really unfortunate if dad continued to get close to Genevieve only to find out she isn't his daughter."

"What did you say, Amir?"

"Has dad mentioned to you if he got a paternity test?" Amir asked.

"No."

"Don't you think he should?"

"Your father's smart. I assumed he already dealt with it."

"I doubt he wants to believe the baby he delivered might not be his."

"Amir, do you really think it's possible Genevieve isn't his daughter?"

"There's only one way to know for sure. You need to tell dad to get a DNA test," Amir assisted.

Talisa looked at her son and then over at Genesis, Skylar, and Genevieve. The photographer was taking a picture of the three of them together like they were one happy family. A family which didn't include her or Amir.

"I think you're right. It's time your father finds out if Genevieve is truly his daughter."

"Baby, I need to take this call," Supreme told Precious, stepping outside on the terrace. "What's going on, Tony?"

"I finally tracked down the woman who was taking care of Arnez."

"You're talking about the woman I saw and paid off before leaving Arnez for dead?" Supreme wanted to confirm.

"Yes. She never went back to the house after the day you saw her. I did ask her for any visitors Arnez had while he was recuperating there."

"And...what did you she tell you?"

"There was only one person. His sister, Astrid."

"Arnez had a sister, a biological sister?"

"Yes. She would come every week, sometimes twice a week," Tony informed Supreme.

"I'll be damned. I had no idea Arnez had a sister. Is she local?"

"The woman wasn't sure. She also didn't know her last name. I did a search on Astrid Douglass, since that was Arnez's last name, but came up empty."

"She had to be the one who was helping

Arnez before he died. If he is in fact still alive, she would be doing the same now."

"Supreme, I've dug as deep as one can go and I haven't found any evidence Arnez is alive. I believe someone started a stupid rumor. There are people who will swear you up and down Tupac is still alive but we know it isn't the case."

'True but this is Arnez we're talking about. I want you to find his sister. Once we hear what she has to say, then I'll know what to do next. Locate this Astrid woman ASAP," Supreme demanded ending the call.

Chapter Eighteen

A Change Is Gonna Come

"I was beginning to think you were avoiding me." Arnez handed Caleb a cold bottled water and sat down across from him with his glass of red wine.

"Why would I do that," Caleb said taking the cap off the bottle. "Our business relationship has been very profitable."

"I feel the same way but lately you've been MIA."

"I've been busy. Once I took over for Khyree, things changed but we knew that would happen," Caleb shrugged.

"True. The other day I had one of my men go to the location you're normally at and you weren't there. None of your crew knew where you were."

"I went to New York for a couple of days," Caleb said but Arnez already knew that. Caleb figured as much, that's why he came clean. He figured Arnez was testing him.

"New York. Why were you in New York?"

"Amir invited me to a get together."

"What kind of get together?"

"Genesis recently had a daughter and there was a family celebration."

"It can't be with Talisa. Is the daughter's mother Skylar?"

"Yeah, that's her name, Skylar. Genesis has her and his kid set up in this dope ass penthouse. That nigga official." Caleb got caught up being hyped over Genesis, he forgot for a second how much Arnez detested the man.

"I see you've jumped on the Genesis band-wagon."

"Nothing like that." Caleb tried playing down his enthusiasm meeting the man he heard so much about but finally met for the very first time. "All I meant, was Genesis got his people living official. I just want to do that for me and mine one day too."

Arnez nodded his head, analyzing the young man he wanted to make his protégé. "If you stick with me, you'll be able to do that and much, much more. Don't forget, I kept my word about your brother. I made it possible for you to be able to take over Khyree's territory and now I'm about to give you even more power."

"How do you plan to do that?"

"I'll be getting rid of Delondo Bryant. Once he's gone, all of Philly is yours."

"You told me Delondo is married to your sister. She doesn't have a problem with you taking him out?"

"Astrid understands family comes first. Her loyalty is with me. I'm having her leave town until I get rid of him which will be soon. Once it happens, you'll be that much closer to having all the money and power you crave."

"Bring it on," Caleb said.

"Glad you're ready, 'cause I plan to. I wanted to run something else by you too."

"What's that?"

"When I first recruited you, I told you how

important it was that you didn't discuss or disclose our relationship with anyone."

"And I haven't."

"Are you sure, because somehow a rumor has surfaced that I'm very much alive."

"It ain't me." Caleb shook his head.

"Then I need you to keep your ear to the street and help me find out who this mystery woman is."

"It's a woman runnin' her mouth?"

"From what I've been told. Again, this is all speculation based on a rumor. But the rumor does have legs and it's bringing some unwanted attention my way."

"If that's true, do you think it's a good idea to have Delondo killed right now? He's a top level mover in Philly. The streets still buzzin' over Khyree. They gon' go crazy over Delondo," Caleb stated.

"Delondo is a necessary kill. Keeping him around will eventually blow my cover. He has to go."

"I'll keep my ears open, try to find out who our here yappin'."

"You do that. I'll maintain a low profile until Delondo's death blows over. By then, with your help, I'll be ready to make my move on Genesis and take him down. I've waited this long. I can be a little more patient."

Arnez continued to sip on his red wine, relishing on the thought of finally outsmarting Genesis and watching his demise.

"Have I told you today how amazing you are?"

"Yes, you told me this morning when we woke up," Talisa smiled, gazing at her husband across the table.

"Did I tell you how beautiful you look in that dress?"

"Well you told me when I tried it on for you before I got dressed for our lunch date this afternoon. But I never get tired of hearing you tell me how amazing I am or how beautiful I look," Talisa beamed.

"That's good because I plan to tell you every day and sometimes even multiple times a day, so you never forget," Genesis promised.

"You get no complaints from me because I plan to do the same thing to my handsome, amazing husband."

"Then we're on the same page," Genesis grinned glancing down at his menu. "Have you decided what you're getting for dessert?"

"Not yet. I'm still a tad full from our lunch. I'm giving my food some time to digest before diving into dessert but I'm definitely getting it. Speaking of dessert, the cake for Genevieve's get together was delicious."

"I'm not even a big fan of cake but it was incredible. It tasted homemade. Next time we have any sort of event, I'm using the same caterer. Everything was delicious. Very impressive."

"I agree. I'm really happy you were pleased with everything."

"All thanks to my beautiful wife."

For the last few days, Talisa had been waiting for the perfect time to have 'the talk' with Genesis. She finally came to the conclusion that there would never be a perfect time. She would just have to do it and Talisa decided it was now or never.

"Baby, I wanted to talk to you about something that has been on my mind."

"Go right ahead," Genesis said as he casually continued glancing over the dessert menu.

"It's about Genevieve."

"My Genevieve, such a beautiful baby girl isn't she?" Genesis proudly said, still not looking up at his wife, but listening.

"Yes, she is beautiful. I can see how much you love her."

"Of course, I do. I brought her into this world. I'll remember the day I delivered her for the rest of my life."

"I'm sure you will. Something that monumental is bound to create an almost unbreakable bond. That's why I strongly believe you should get a DNA test before you become even more attached."

"Excuse me?" those words his wife spoke, certainly diverted Genesis's eyes away from the menu and he stared directly into Talisa's face.

"You have completely given your heart to a baby you're not one hundred percent sure is yours."

"Where is this coming from, Talisa? How do you know I haven't had a paternity test?"

"Have you had a paternity test?" Talisa asked point blank. The uncomfortable silence answered her question. "That would be a no."

"I don't need a test. I know Genevieve is my daughter. If I wasn't positive, I wouldn't have named her after my sister."

"Why are you so positive...because Skylar said so? She isn't the embodiment of honesty and trustworthy."

"Is that what this is about...her leaving you on the island? Yes, Skylar was wrong but in the end, she did the right thing and told the truth. Don't punish Genevieve for the mistake her mother made."

"Is that what you think? I would try to punish an innocent child due to my dislike for her mother. I thought you knew me better than that, Genesis."

"I just don't understand why you're doing this, Talisa. I thought you had embraced Genevieve. Why did you put together that beautiful event for my daughter if you hadn't yet accepted her?"

"I did it because I love you more than anything in this world. I want to love and accept Genevieve too but only after you are positive she's your daughter. You should want the same thing too. If this was Amir, you would demand he have a DNA test before the baby even left the hospital. Why aren't you demanding the same for yourself? Is it because you're still in love with Skylar and you only want to see the good in her?"

Genesis breathed heavily, rubbing his eyes while putting his head down. "I'll have the test done, Talisa. I'll set up everything with Skylar today. And for the record, you're the only woman I'm in love with. That's the only reason I'm agreeing to have this paternity test done because in my heart, I know Genevieve is my daughter."

"Thank you," Talisa said stoically.

"I won't be having any dessert. I lost my appetite. Are you ready to go?" Although Genesis asked his wife the question, by his demeanor it came across as more of a demand.

"Yes, I'm ready." Talisa grabbed her purse and followed Genesis out the restaurant. She tried not to take his cold attitude personally. Talisa knew she was diving head first into murky water by even bringing the topic up to her husband. But in her heart, she knew it had to be done. Talisa prayed her request wouldn't cause irreparable damage to her marriage.

Chapter Nineteen

Bad Liar

Caleb and Floyd were riding through every neighborhood he had workers posted in. Caleb had lieutenants within his crew who could easily take care of that including Floyd, but he preferred to do it himself. Caleb was a person who preferred to micromanage everything. He didn't trust that anyone could make sure his operation was running to his liking but him. Due to his need to triple check everything, it made him extremely successful with his growing drug operation but it also left little time for him to have a life outside of moving drugs.

"Who the fuck is this that keeps calling me?" Caleb said with irritation while turning down the block.

"If you answer the phone you would know," Floyd cracked.

"Did I ask for yo' opinion, smart ass?" Caleb chuckled. "Oh I see the dummy wised up and decided to send a text," he said glancing down at his phone.

Caleb it's me, Mia. Please call me. It's an emergency!!

"Fuck! I hope ain't nothing happen to my niece," Caleb muttered out loud pulling over to the side of the street.

"Something wrong wit' Amelia?" Floyd asked with concern.

"Not sure. It was Mia blowin' up my phone. She sent me a text sayin' it's an emergency," Caleb explained to Floyd while calling Mia back.

"Hey!" Mia answered.

"Is Amelia okay?" Was all Caleb wanted to know.

"Yes! Amelia is fine. This isn't about her."

"Then what's up wit' you blowin' up my

phone and sending me a text sayin' it's an emergency?!" Caleb didn't even bother trying to camouflage his annoyance with Mia.

"I overheard something you need to know about," Mia said coyly.

"This shit better be good."

"I really don't want to tell you over the phone. Can we meet up?"

"Tell me the shit now or keep it to yo' fuckin' self," Caleb spat.

"This guy who used to work for Khyree but now works for Delondo is planning on killing you."

"Huh?! What's the nigga's name?" Caleb didn't believe Mia would make something like this up but he had to be sure she knew what the fuck she was talking about.

"His name is Martel but he goes by Mack on the streets."

When Mia dropped the name, Caleb knew it was highly likely her intel was legit.

"Where you at?"

"Home."

"Stay there. I'm on the way."

"Going somewhere?"

"Delondo, you scared me." Astrid looked up and saw her husband standing in the doorway of their bedroom. "I thought you were going to be in Maryland for a couple days." She dropped the shirt she was about to put in her suitcase.

"I cut my trip short. Good thing I did since it appears my wife is leaving me."

"You're so silly," Astrid laughed nervously. "While you were gone, I was going to stay at the Ritz Carlton for a couple days while I get a spa treatment. Pamper myself a little bit."

"You're taking a lot of clothes for a couple of days. Where's Delilah?"

"With the nanny."

"I see." Delondo came towards Astrid who was at the foot of the bed. "You wouldn't be lying to me, would you?" he asked lifting her hair up off her shoulders.

"Of course not." Astrid could barely maintain eye contact with her husband.

"You didn't ask me why I cut my trip short."

"I didn't have a chance."

"Now you do. So, ask me."

"Why did you cut your trip short?" Astrid's voice wavered.

"Because I got a call from Renny. He was in

New York on his way to come see me in Philly. We decided to meet up in Maryland."

Delondo was speaking the words Astrid knew her husband was going to say but it didn't stop her from dreading to hear them. She knew the gig was up, she only wondered what all Renny spilled about her and if she could lie her way out any of it.

"Really, what did Renny want to see you about?" Astrid did her best to conjure up a poker face but it wasn't in the cards.

"You. Imagine my surprise when Renny informed me I was married to the sister of my worst enemy." Delondo moved his hands from Astrid's hair to her bare neck.

"When we met, I had no idea of your history with Arnez."

"You lying bitch. I know it was you workin' wit' Theron before his snitch ass got murked. That means you was workin' wit' Arnez snake ass!"

"No! No!" Astrid denied.

"Renny came wit' receipts thanks to T-Roc so save yo' fuckin' lies!"

"Arnez forced me! He said he would kill me, you and Delilah if I didn't' help him. I was trying to protect my family!" Astrid cried.

"I only have one question for you. Is Arnez really dead or is he alive?"

"Dead. I swear!" she said convincingly.

"I can't believe shit that comes out yo' fuckin' mouth. You've been tellin' me nothin' but lies on top of lies. Because of you and Theron, I could've been locked up by the feds. You dead to me!" Delondo barked as he began choking the life out of Astrid.

"Don't do this. What about Delilah..." Astrid struggled to say as her body began to fall to the bed.

Delondo's eyes locked with Astrid's and he could see the fear, desperation, and life leaving her body. He thought about the little girl he adored more than anything and having to explain her mother was dead. He softened his grip on Astrid. For the brief second he changed his mind she took advantage and went into survival mode.

Astrid reached for the lamp on the night-stand next to the bed and slammed it over Delondo's head as hard as she could. Instead of falling backwards to the floor, his heavy body fell on top of hers. Astrid did her best to wriggle from underneath him. When she finally managed to maneuver her body free, Delondo started to come to.

"Get yo' ass back over here! You fuckin' dead!" Delondo howled pulling her leg as she scrambled to jump across the bed.

"Stooooop!" Astrid yelled but Delondo had regained the majority of his strength and there was no stopping him. When she turned back and saw the hate in his eyes, she knew there wouldn't be a next time. He was gonna finish her ass off.

"You ain't got nowhere to run. I'ma kill you." Delondo stated as if her body was already at the morgue. But Astrid wasn't ready to die. She remembered Delondo kept a gun in the nightstand on his side of the bed, in the upper drawer. She leaped over there like her life depended on it and it did. She got hold of the gun and, without hesitation, she unleashed those bullets into her husband's face and chest until he was dead.

"You think Mack really tryna have you killed?" Floyd was finding it difficult to believe the shit since Mack seemed somewhat soft to him.

"He wasn't too thrilled when I cut him off after I took over for Khyree. A few of them niggas was pissy."

"They brought that shit on themselves. Them

cats was lazy. Khyree didn't give a fuck 'cause he won't payin' them shit no way. You did right not carryin' all that dead weight," Floyd scoffed.

"You know it and I know it but Mack and them other clowns might be out for some retribution type shit. What I can't understand is why Delondo would put him on with his crew," Caleb said as they pulled up in front of Mia's crib.

"Maybe Delondo thought gettin' somebody who used to be in Khyree's inner circle, would be able to give him some insight on how we conduct our business. Mack is lazy but the nigga could talk a good game," Floyd said.

"True dat. Hold on, here come Mia." Caleb eyed her intently while she walked towards his car.

Floyd turned in the direction Caleb nodded his head. "Man, this chick bet not be talkin' crazy."

"Hey, Caleb. I'm glad you came over. Can you get out the car so we can talk?" Mia asked.

"Whatever we discuss can be said in front of Floyd."

"Okay." Mia seemed disappointed but telling Caleb what she knew, was most important to her.

"First thing I want you to tell me, is how you know Mack?"

"I don't..."

Caleb and Floyd both rolled their eyes up and sighed, shaking their head. "Here we go wit' the bullshit," Floyd huffed.

"If you don't know Mack, how you so sure he tryna kill me?"

"I don't know him but Celinda does," Mia stuttered.

"Celinda!" Floyd howled. "Man, what that girl mixed up in now?"

"Let me guess, Celinda fuckin' wit' the dude Mack." Caleb gritted his teeth. "Which means Prevan dumbass is runnin' his fuckin' mouth to this trick."

"Damn!" Floyd sunk down in the passenger seat. "Prevan done fucked up now."

"I hate even bringing Celinda into this but this your life we are talking about," Mia said. "Yes, Celinda is messing with Mack. Yesterday she thought I left her apartment but I came back because I forgot something. Her and Mack were in her bedroom. They just finished having sex and were smoking weed. I heard Mack mention your name so I started ear hustling."

"What did the nigga say?" Caleb was pressed to hear.

"He started talking about some Arnez guy. Saying he still couldn't believe Celinda told him

Arnez was alive and you were working with him. She told Mack it was all true and that's how you were able to get Prevan out of jail because you made a deal with Arnez."

A migraine instantly kicked Caleb in the head. He now was one hundred percent sure Mia was telling the truth. Although he had told Arnez he hadn't discussed their arrangement with anyone, he wasn't being honest. He told Floyd and his brother. He knew Floyd wouldn't tell a soul but Prevan was a weak ass when it came to his baby mother.

"When is he supposed to be tryna take me out?" Caleb asked.

"I didn't hear him tell my sister a specific time but I had to leave. They were coming out the bedroom and I couldn't let them see me there. All I heard him say was that he and Delondo's people were going to take you out and he would end up being Delondo's second in command."

"Floyd, give me some money," Caleb told him. Caleb always let Floyd hold the majority of what he called play cash when they were rolling the streets together. Play cash to Caleb was more than most people's one month salary.

"How much?" Floyd wanted to know.

"All of it."

Floyd emptied his pockets and Caleb handed the money over to Mia. "Thank you."

"I don't want your money," Mia said pushing his hand away. "I didn't tell you this to get paid. I told you because I don't want you to die."

"I appreciate that but take the money. If you don't, I'ma leave it in your mailbox and somebody else gonna end up takin' it. Better you than them."

Mia hesitated for a second but eventually took the money. "Please be careful out here, Caleb. And please don't hurt Celinda. I know she doesn't make the best decisions but she is my sister and Amelia needs her mother."

"I ain't gon' touch Celinda. I'ma leave that up to Prevan. But what we discussed stays between us. Got it?"

"Got it. Call me if you need me, Caleb." Mia stood on the sidewalk and watched as he drove off.

"Man, that girl got it so bad for you, I almost feel sorry for her," Floyd laughed. "She really didn't want to take yo' money neither. Bless her," Floyd joked and continued laughing.

"I know."

"Why you insist she take it?"

"Because I didn't want her thinking I owed her anything. If I didn't pay her wit' money, then I would have to pay her with my time. I don't have nothing to give her emotionally. Money is the next best thing."

"I feel you. So, what's our next move? We have to strike before Mack has a chance," Floyd stated.

"Indeed, we do. We'll start at the top and work our way down," Caleb nodded.

Caleb never considered himself a killer per se, but he was a strong believer in self-preservation. He knew Arnez was planning on taking Delondo out but he decided he would speed up the process and do it himself. After getting rid of the man at the top, everyone else would soon fall.

Chapter Twenty

Turning Point

"My beautiful, Genevieve!" Skylar cooed over her daughter while gently brushing her hair. "Daddy will be here soon and we want you to look picture perfect."

Skylar held her daughter up and was pleased with her attire. She put Genevieve in a pink cotton blend footed coverall, with a Peter Pan collar. It was a snap on style with the multicolored print of the Fendi label's signature cartoon characters.

"This is perfect! Your Godmother has such great taste!" Skylar smiled, loving the gift Precious got for Genevieve. While Skylar continued gushing over her baby girl, she heard the door. "I bet that's your daddy!"

"There's my favorite girl!" Genesis beamed when Skylar opened the door and saw his daughter. "Look at that smile! I missed you too." He reached out, taking Genevieve from Skylar's arms.

"She always gets the biggest smile when you come around," Skylar remarked, closing the door. "Can I get you something to drink?"

"No, I'm good. I have everything I need right here." Genesis sat down, holding Genevieve as she looked up at him. Her eyes seemed to sparkle while she made squealing sounds. "I love you so much," he kept saying while staring at her.

"She's getting so big," Skylar grinned.

"Yes, she is and just beautiful. Daddy's little girl. Skylar, I need to speak with you about something and I don't want you to take it the wrong way."

"Okay. You sound super serious."

"I mean there's no easy way of saying this, so I'll just say it. I want to get a paternity test for Genevieve."

"What! Where is this coming from? After all this time, you decide you want a paternity test. You signed the birth certificate!" Skylar yelled.

"I know because there is no doubt in my mind this beautiful little girl is mine. But..."

"But what?!" Skylar screamed, cutting Genesis off.

"I understand you're upset but please don't yell in front of Genevieve," Genesis said laying her on his chest.

"If you believe Genevieve's your daughter then why the DNA test? Let me guess, Talisa." Skylar shook her head. "I know she put you up to this," she accused him angrily.

"This has nothing to do with Talisa," Genesis lied. "I should've got a test done initially."

"This has everything to do with Talisa! If you wanted a paternity test then you would've gotten one right after our daughter was born. You and I both know she's your child. I can't believe you would ask this of me." Skylar's anger now turned to tears of pain.

"Skylar, please don't cry." Genesis got up and walked over to her with Genevieve in his arms. The guilt was taking a toll on him. Even though he wouldn't admit it to Skylar, she was right. If it wasn't for Talisa, he would've never asked for a paternity test, that's how sure he was that Genevieve was his.

"What do you expect for me to do, Genesis? Smile and pretend I'm not hurt. This isn't the ideal situation for me. You know I'm still in love with you and I always imagined we would raise our daughter together as a family. I've accepted that's not going to happen but this is such a blow."

"I'm sorry. Please let's just get this done. The sooner we do, we can put it behind us. I'll make it up to you...I promise." Genesis put his arm around Skylar and kissed her on the forehead.

"I spoke to Justina last night. She mentioned to me you called her."

"Can't a father call his daughter?" T-Roc replied keeping his eyes glued to his made to order, Stuart Hudges Prestige HD Supreme Edition television. Ever since he purchased the limited edition set covered with nineteen kilograms of gold along with 50 pieces of diamonds, it monopolized all his attention when in their master suite. The sinfully expensive gadget was T-Roc's personal trophy piece.

"You can call your daughter but you don't

have to interrogate her," Chantal countered.

Per usual, T-Roc didn't have much to say as he laid back in the Majesty Vi-spring bed staring at what had become like an in house mistress. Chantal was growing impatient. She wanted her husband's full attention but he had none to give. She got up from the chair and stood directly in front of the television.

"What you doing?" the baffled glare on T-Roc's face made Chantal even more incensed.

"I'm trying to have a conversation with you about our daughter but you give that fuckin' television more attention then you give your own wife!"

"It's not my fault the television has found a way to hold my attention unlike my wife."

Chantal was used to her husband's cold and sometimes cruel lingo, so what he said rolled right off her back. Her lack of caring was one of the main reasons T-Roc did have little to no interest in his wife.

"Justina can tell you're questioning her for a reason and it isn't simply a father checking on his daughter. You need to either just spit out what you have to say or leave it alone." T-Roc remained silent. "If you don't open yo' motherfuckin' mouth and say something, I'ma take my heel," Chantal threatened, snatching off her shoe, "And smash this damn TV. Keep ignoring me if you fuckin' like!"

The more upset Chantal became, her arms were moving around erratically, causing the straps on the negligee she was wearing to start falling off her shoulders. Although the two of them basically had a sexless marriage, Chantal loved to look sexy. Not for her husband but for herself, which pissed T-Roc off but also turned him on. As crazy and neurotic as Chantal could be, there was no denying she was still a breathtaking beauty.

"That's a one-point-five-million-dollar television. If you smash it, I will break your neck," T-Roc warned.

Chantal didn't seem to give a flying fuck about T-Roc's threat. She raised her arm as if she was about to swing down with her heel, hitting the television directly in the center of the screen. Chantal's craziness was legendary, so T-Roc didn't want to take any chances she would follow through on her threat.

"Okay, Chantal!" T-Roc jumped out of bed and said. "I'll handle the situation with Justina. I'm having a difficult time processing the extent of which our daughter was involved with Arnez and

Maya. I'm concerned about her mental wellbeing. Honestly, I'm afraid." T-Roc hated to admit. He thought if he didn't talk about what Justina had done, maybe he could keep suppressing his feelings

"Finally!" Chantal raised her arms rejoicing. "You're showing some real emotions instead of the cold exterior you constantly portray. I was beginning to wonder if you even gave a damn," she folded her arms and said.

"Of course, I give a damn!" T-Roc fired back. "My family means everything to me. You included, believe it or not."

At first T-Roc regretted proclaiming the last part to his wife. Their marriage had been more so about keeping up appearances than commitment for the last few years. T-Roc knew Chantal was well aware of his indiscretions but she seemed to have become numb to it. On the other hand, although he never admitted it to his wife, he was devastated about her relationship with Lorenzo. Chantal was unaware, but once it ended, T-Roc kept one of his security detail monitoring her every move. He wanted to make sure he stopped Chantal from entering into another fling with a man before it even had a chance to start.

"You have a strange way of showing your

family, me included, mean everything to you." Chantal's eyes darted off in another direction not wanting her face to reveal she cared about what T-Roc divulged.

"I do." T-Roc placed his hand on Chantal's shoulder. It seemed like forever since he touched her skin. It had this silky feeling where his fingers could glide right off. He wrapped his muscular arms around her waist, as his bare chest pressed against her warm body.

"You haven't held me like this in so long," Chantal whispered.

"Because I knew you didn't want me to." T-Roc lifted her chin so their eyes could lock. "Has that changed?"

Instead of answering his question, Chantal leaned in and placed her lips against his. Their tongues intertwined and soon the lovemaking began. The physical attraction and chemistry between them had never left. T-Roc licked, kissed, thrusted, pressed, and pounded every inch of his wife's body and she savored each second of it. It had been so long since Chantal had felt her husband inside of her, she had forgotten how he had a way of hypnotizing her with the dick. He made it feel like the first time.

If for only one night, T-Roc and Chantal

were able to subdue their fear and uncertainty about Justina's future and simply get lost in their passion for each other.

"Amir, what a pleasant surprise. I wasn't expecting you to come over today." Talisa gave him a hug, happy to see her son.

"It's good to see you too." Amir sat down at the kitchen table while Talisa poured them something to drink. "I actually came over to see dad. I needed to discuss some business with him," he said taking the glass from his mother.

"I see. I guess your father didn't tell you he and Skylar were getting the paternity test done today," Talisa disclosed.

"No! I didn't even think you mentioned it to him yet."

"I did, a few days after the party I put together. We were having lunch and I finally worked up the nerves to mention it."

"Based on your expression, it didn't go over well," Amir said.

"It didn't. Your father has been so distant ever since I brought it up. I'm just glad they're getting the test done, so we can get the results and try to move past this. I don't know if we can though," Talisa shrugged.

"Why do you say that?"

"He seems resentful. As if he blames me for asking him to have the test done. Last night we got in an argument and he was defending Skylar like she was a victim. He's convinced Genevieve is his daughter and I'm afraid when the test comes back confirming that, it's only going to strengthen his relationship with Skylar."

"Things are that bad?" Amir couldn't help but be concerned.

"Unfortunately, they are," Talisa admitted, sadly. "Genesis is in love with that baby. I basically forced him to have a paternity test done and now I feel like an outsider. Him, Skylar and Genevieve, then me. I'm sure Skylar is taking full advantage of this."

"I'm so, so sorry, Mom. I should've never had you go to dad and ask him to get a paternity test done." Amir shook his head.

"You have nothing to apologize for. You didn't force me to speak to your father. Honestly, it had always been in the back of my mind but I figured Genesis would request a DNA test on his own. I think delivering Skylar's baby blurred his judgment."

"Mom, I can see the stress all over your face." Amir went over to his mother and hugged her.

"I don't want to lose your father but I can't compete with a beautiful little baby girl and I shouldn't have to."

"And you won't. You have to stay optimistic. You know how much dad loves you. This will pass. I promise."

Talisa welcomed Amir's kind words and prayed what her son said would turn out to be true.

Chapter Twenty-One

Misery Lives Here

"You sure this a good idea?" Floyd questioned as Caleb turned onto the cul-de-sac where Delondo lived.

"Arnez had mentioned Delondo was going to be in Maryland for a few days. This is the perfect time for us to scope out his crib. Figure out the best way to get in and take him out when we're ready to make our move."

"Delondo, mos def stackin' some major paper,

'cause these cribs over here are ridiculous." Floyd exclaimed looking around at the neighboring houses.

"Fo' sure. That's why it'll be easy to make it seem like a home invasion gone wrong by killin' him at his crib. An upscale neighborhood like this is a prime location for thieves," Caleb reasoned.

"You got a point there."

"There's his crib right there," Caleb nodded.

"It look mad dark over there, like ain't nobody home."

"Because there isn't. That's why we here," Caleb scoffed parking down the street. "Now let's go take a look around. Put yo' hoodie up, just in case anybody watching, they can't see our faces."

Luckily it was the dead of night, the street was quiet and not another person in sight. Caleb and Floyd made their way to Delondo's property without detection.

"Let's go around the back," Caleb said. "There might be an easy entrance."

"It can't be easier than an open front door," Floyd popped heading up the front stairs.

"Hold up! Where you going?"

"You don't see that shit?! The front door is slightly ajar," Floyd said in a loud, whispered tone. "We mind as well go take a look inside."

Caleb was reluctant but his curiosity had him follow Floyd inside. "This shit don't feel right," Caleb said.

"Don't worry, I'm packin'."

"Nigga, I'm not. Glad ain't nobody here." Caleb felt defenseless walking in somebody's house unarmed even if nobody was home.

"This place is sweet. I like them winding stairs," Floyd commented walking up.

"Where you going?" Caleb shouted.

"Just checking the place out."

"I'ma go take a look in the back. Don't get lost up there," Caleb cracked.

Caleb needed to turn a light on so bad, in order to get a clear layout of the house but he didn't want to bring any unwanted attention, since he and Floyd were already breaking the law. Not only that, in the back of his mind, he still wondered why the front door was left open. *Maybe somebody was in a rush and accidently left it open when they were leaving, Caleb* thought to himself walking towards a wall of large windows overlooking the outdoor pool.

While Caleb analyzed the door leading outside to the pool, to see if it would be easy to pick the lock, he had no idea he was being watched. Astrid had come back in the house because she'd forgotten her purse in the kitchen, after putting the last of the belongings she was taking with her in the car. Before Astrid could exit back out through the garage, she heard someone come in the house. She panicked and took cover in one of the closets downstairs.

I can't believe I left the front door open, Astrid yelled to herself, cracking open the closet door. The moonlight shining through the windows gave her a clear shot at what appeared to be a tall, medium built guy, wearing some jeans and a hoodie. When Caleb kneeled down to examine the lock on the door, he pushed back his hood and Astrid got a side view of his face. *He looks young, no more than nineteen and he doesn't appear to have a weapon*, Astrid thought, which gave her an idea.

She reached in her purse and retrieved the gun she used to kill her husband. Astrid figured the teenage boy was looking to rob the place and would run in fear, if he felt the tip of a gun pointed at his back. Astrid waited patiently until Caleb finished whatever he was doing in the living room area and walked past the closet she was hiding in. Once he did, she made her move.

"Get the fuck out my house or I will blow your head off!" Astrid threatened. Caleb heard the gun cock as Astrid pressed the barrel in his back.

"I don't want no problems," Caleb said putting his hands up walking towards the door as Astrid pressed the gun even harder in his back.

"Stop running your mouth! Maybe a bullet in your brain will shut you up!" Astrid had now moved the gun from Caleb's back to his head.

"Lady, please don't shoot me!" Caleb had a bad feeling about coming into this house and now he feared he was about to lose his life behind his reckless decision. "Don't shoot!" he yelled one more time before he heard a gunshot go off and closed his eyes thinking his life over.

When a few seconds went by and Caleb didn't have any pain or the feeling like a bomb went off inside his chest or being jack-hammered through his brain, he realized he hadn't been shot. But there was no relief because Caleb did hear a gun fire and he wondered if maybe the woman somehow missed. He decided to dive down to the floor in case she tried to shoot him again.

"Caleb, are you okay?!" Floyd yelled out, running down the stairs.

"I'm straight," Caleb said getting up. "Was it you that shot the gun?"

There was no need for Floyd to respond

because Caleb saw Astrid's body lying in a pool of blood.

"Man, you lucky I got a good shot. I was scared I might accidently hit you, that's why I only fired once," Floyd said standing over Astrid's body.

"She's dead." Caleb shook his head after he checked for a pulse. "I think this might be Arnez's sister, Astrid," he sighed.

"If that's her, then I'm betting she's the one who killed her husband."

"Wait...what?! Delondo is dead?"

"Yeah! While I was being a nosey mother-fucker upstairs, I came across his dead body in their bedroom. I wasn't sure at first because half of his face was missing." Floyd shook his head in disgust thinking about how foul the shit looked. "But I checked his wallet, to see if the dead man had any ID. The driver's license said Delondo."

"Fuck! We need to get the hell outta here. We ain't 'bout to get caught in this house wit' two dead bodies," Caleb barked as the two men made their exit.

Genesis was on his way to a meeting when he got the phone call regarding the paternity results.

Instead of continuing with his initial plans, he had his driver turnaround and head to Skylar's place. He needed to see and hold Genevieve.

When Genesis knocked, Skylar seemed to be awaiting his arrival as she opened the door immediately. "Where's Genevieve?"

"In the living room." Skylar said, closing the door. She followed behind Genesis and watched as he reached in the playpen and got her.

"You have the most beautiful eyes, Genevieve. They always sparkle," Genesis smiled as Genevieve smiled back. "Although I'm not your father, I will always love you and will cherish the time we spent together." A tear rolled down Genesis's cheek holding the baby girl he never knew he could love so much.

Skylar broke down and began to bawl. Her world was literally about to crash down around her. She thought losing Genesis to Talisa was painful, losing him as her baby daddy almost felt worse than death. Seeing him say his final goodbyes to the little girl he delivered into this world was too much for Skylar to bear. She ran to her bedroom, desperate to escape what was to come next...Genesis being out of her life forever.

It took a few more minutes but when Skylar lifted her face from sobbing in her pillow, she noticed Genesis standing in her bedroom doorway.

"Genesis..."

"Save it." Genesis put up his hand. "I never thought I could loathe anyone as much as I did Arnez before he died but you proved me wrong. I might actually detest you more."

"You don't mean that," Skylar cried.

"But I do. You allowed me to completely give my heart to a baby you knew wasn't mine. That has to be the cruelest thing anyone can do to another human being."

"I swear, I thought Genevieve was yours! I was only with one other man and it's when I was trying to escape the island. I did whatever I had to do, so I could get back home to you. There was no way I thought the universe could be so heartless by allowing that man to be the father of my beautiful baby."

"Clearly the universe hates you just as much as I do."

Genesis's statement sent Skylar spiraling back into despair. "I'm so sorry!" she wailed. "You have to believe me, I never thought this would happen."

"I do believe you and it wouldn't have if it wasn't for my wife. Thank goodness Talisa wasn't blinded by love the way I was. Genevieve had become my world and I threw caution out the window. If she hadn't insisted I get a paternity test, you would've let this lie go on forever."

"Genesis, please. You can still be a father to Genevieve. She needs you!" Skylar pleaded.

"You're sick. I'm giving you ninety days to vacate this property and it's only because I do still love Genevieve and I want to make sure she's okay. All the money I've given you thus far, should be more than enough for you to leave New York and start your life over someplace else. But I want you to stay away from me. Don't ever contact me again, Skylar. You are dead to me."

"Genesis wait!" she wailed running behind him, all the way until he reached the door. Skylar was on the floor holding on to the bottom of his pants, trying to keep him for leaving. Her sobs grew louder and louder to the point that baby Genevieve began crying too.

"Get a hold of yourself!" Genesis barked. "You have a child to take care of. Grow the fuck up and be a mother to your daughter. Genevieve needs you but I don't." Genesis pushed Skylar off his leg and slammed the door in her face, leaving her to drown in her own misery.

Chapter Twenty-Two

Moving On

"This is an unexpected surprise," Supreme said to T-Roc when he got out his car. They both pulled up to Delondo's house at the same time.

"Unexpected surprise would be right. I had no idea you were friends with Delondo."

"I'm not." Supreme walked over to where T-Roc was standing. "I'm not here to see Delondo. I'm here to see Astrid."

"Really. How do you know Delondo's wife?"

T-Roc was doing his best to come across in a casual relaxed tone. He didn't want to raise any suspicion. Supreme and T-Roc weren't enemies but they also weren't going out for drinks together. Although having dinner together wasn't out the question, neither was each other's first choice. So, T-Roc wanted to play it close to the vest but still find out what brought him Philly to see Astrid.

"I don't know her either. But it was recently brought to my attention that she's the sister of a person we mutually know," Supreme stated.

"You must mean Arnez." T-Roc said as if he had nothing to hide. "I recently found out the same thing. I came to speak to Delondo about it. Anything that has to do with Arnez concerns me because of Genesis."

T-Roc and Supreme weren't besties but both were close to Genesis, so T-Roc knew his explanation would resonate with Supreme. There was no way T-Roc would admit he also came to see Astrid but it was to find out how deep her relationship ran with his daughter Justina. Renny had told him he already spoke to Delondo and he was in Maryland for a few days. T-Roc thought this was the perfect time to swoop in and speak to his wife, while she was home alone. Running into Supreme was throwing an unforeseen complication in his plans.

"Since we're here for basically the same reason, let's go knock on the door and speak to Mr. & Mrs. Bryant. I'll let you lead the way since you're cool with the man of the house," Supreme smiled.

T-Roc smiled back at Supreme but it was all fake. This was the main reason the two would never be but so close, they were too much alike. T-Roc hated that Supreme was equally as arrogant, confident, and rich as him. What pissed T-Roc off even more was Supreme was unbelievably smart and was a master of masking his true feelings. Supreme would allow you to believe one thing and you'd never know he was plotting something else until after his plan had been fully executed.

"That's strange," T-Roc said when he got to the top of the stairs.

"What is?"

"The door's open," T-Roc told him.

"I'm packin', how 'bout you?"

"Yep." T-Roc nodded.

"Then let's go in." Supreme said, pushing the door wide open. That's when they saw the first dead body. "Damn. I'm assuming that's Astrid?"

"Yeah, it is." T-Roc remembered what she looked like when he met her a few months ago with Delondo.

"She has a gun in her hand. She was prepared to take somebody out but she got before she could get them. Let's take a look around the rest of the house."

"Okay, you look down here and I'll look around upstairs," T-Roc suggested.

"Cool."

When T-Roc got upstairs he got an unnerving feeling. He walked past Delilah's bedroom first. He was relieved he didn't see the little girl lying dead in her bed but he couldn't shake the eerie mood. He knew why when came up to the master bedroom and saw a man's dead body. At first T-Roc didn't know what to think. Was this some other man Astrid was creeping with on the low, while Delondo was out of town? Whoever came in the house, did they get him too? All these thoughts were running around T-Roc's mind.

"Fuck!" T-Roc mumbled, when got close to the body and half of his face had been blown away. He didn't want to believe it, but based on his body build, complexion and the tattoo on his arm, T-Roc knew it had to be Delondo. He saw a wallet lying next to the body as if somebody had gone through it. The driver license was on the floor and when he picked it up, his thoughts were confirmed.

"Everything is clear downstairs, did you find anything upstairs?!" T-Roc heard Supreme call out.

"Yeah! I'm in the last bedroom down the hall."

"Damn! Another dead body," Supreme said when he got to the bedroom and saw T-Roc sitting down on a chair.

"It's Delondo. He was a good dude. I can't believe he's dead." T-Roc kept shaking his head. "Renny and Lorenzo gon' take this shit hard."

"Who would want both of them dead?" Supreme wondered out loud.

"I want to know the same thing. Shit just keep gettin' crazier." T-Roc sat dumbfounded.

Supreme and T-Roc both thought they would show up to Delondo's house and get answers, instead they hit another dead end.

"Genesis, you're home," Talisa said glancing over at Amir who had come over to see his mother.

"Dad, are you okay?" Amir stood up. "You

seem upset." Genesis's red, watery eyes were a tell-tale sign that he wasn't.

"Genevieve isn't my daughter. Skylar played me and stomped all over my heart in the process."

Genesis wanted to reveal the truth, embrace his pain and move the fuck on. It was the only way he believed there was a chance he would heal.

"Dad, I'm sorry."

"I am too," Talisa chimed in and said. "I know how much you love Genevieve and it breaks my heart to see you so hurt," she said sincerely.

"I don't want to think about it. Go pack your clothes," Genesis told his wife.

"Huh?" Talisa looked over at Amir and then back at Genesis. "Pack for what?"

"I already had our reservations booked. We're going on a trip around the world. We're leaving today."

"Genesis, are you sure? That's so soon. I mean I would love to go but are you sure you're ready? What about business?" Talisa questioned.

"Amir, can handle business. Right, Amir?"

"Of course." Amir nodded. "Whatever you need, dad. You and mom go have a wonderful trip. The two of you need to get away and spend some alone time together. I'll make sure business runs smoothly while you're gone."

"Please give my apologies to Aaliyah for not being able to attend her wedding. I'll have you pick up her gift before you leave for Miami."

"Aaliyah will understand but I will make sure to tell her."

"Thank you, son. I love you." Genesis wrapped his arms around Amir, feeling blessed he had at least one child that was his.

"You still haven't gotten in touch with Astrid?" Arnez asked one of his hired goons.

"No, we haven't been able to reach her."

"Did you drive by her house?"

"No. We didn't want Delondo getting suspicious. Especially since you want us to make our move against him next week."

"Fuck that nigga. Go to her house and find out what's going on with my sister. If Delondo gets in your way, kill him on the spot. It's not like Astrid to just vanish."

"Mr. Douglass, I think you should see this," Fatima said to Arnez, coming outside to the terrace.

Arnez went inside the house and saw the

television turned to the news. His mouth dropped when he saw the multiple police cars and emergency crews outside what looked like the home his sister and Delondo shared together. When the newscaster revealed the identities of the two dead bodies found inside, Arnez was devastated.

"Change of plans," Arnez informed his goon. "We're moving on that ASAP."

"Skylar, Skylar, girl you have fucked up in the most major way," Precious said, crossing her legs and twirling one of the curls in her hair around her index finger. "How you go from having the best baby daddy ever to no baby daddy at all, in less than twenty-four hours?" she asked shaking her head back and forth.

"Precious, I really don't need you rubbing this shit in. It's already taking every ounce of strength I have not to have a nervous breakdown. Genevieve is the only reason I'm keeping it together...but barely."

"I apologize. I'm glad you're staying strong for Genevieve. She does need her mother. Now more than ever, since she ain't got no daddy."

Skylar rolled her eyes, regretting she invited

Precious over. She needed a friend's shoulder to cry on but Precious wasn't the type of friend to cosign on bullshit. She would let you cry but call your ass out while you're doing it.

"Precious, I fucked up! I get it but can you please help me come up with a solution," Skylar pleaded.

"Oh, I didn't know that's what you called me over for." Precious raised an eyebrow. "I mean, baby girl what sort of solution are you tryna get? We ain't got much to work with. Genesis ain't the father. There's nothing we can do about that. We can't get a redo," she shrugged.

"So, you think I should let him hate me and fade into oblivion?"

"Skylar, listen. I get why you did what you did. You wanted Genevieve to have a wonderful, loving, and rich father. You took a gamble and instead of getting a winner you ended up with a loser as the baby daddy. It can happen to the best of us. But when you gamble, you have to know when to cut your losses. As your friend, I'm telling you, that time has arrived. Let Genesis go. You all were bonded because you shared a child together, that bond has been broken. There's nothing left for you here."

"I built a life here and now it's over," Skylar

said sadly.

"I know it's hard. My goodness," Precious said looking around. "Having to leave this penthouse would make any woman want to slit her wrist. But downsizing could be a good thing. On a positive note, at least Genevieve is still a baby and hasn't grown accustomed to living in all this luxury," she sighed.

"You're making my life sound so bleak. Are you even going to be Genevieve's Godmother anymore?"

"Skylar, how could you even ask such a question. I love that little baby. I didn't agree to be her Godmother because Genesis was the father. I did it because we're friends and I love you. Just because a person fucks up doesn't mean you turn your back on them. Hell, I've fucked up the majority of my life. Thank goodness for second chances and third, fourth, fifth...you get it," Precious laughed and Skylar joined in.

"I was beginning to regret inviting you over but now I'm glad I did. You always end up saying exactly what I need to hear." Skylar gave Precious a huge hug. "Thank you for being a friend."

"Always. I know I've cracked a lot of jokes since I've been here but seriously, how are you financially? I'll be more than happy to give you whatever you need to get a new place, pay some bills, keep food on the table so you and Genevieve ain't over here starving. I'm not gonna leave you out here without a lifeline," Precious made clear.

"You really are amazing but I'm good. Genesis paid all the bills and in the last few months, he's given me enough money where I wouldn't need to work for at least the next year if I didn't want to. Of course, not penthouse money," Skylar clarified, "but enough to figure out what to do with my life. He also gave me ninety days to leave."

"Genesis is the gift that keeps on giving. He has got to be the best baby daddy ever. Sorry I keep reminding you of that." Precious frowned. "After all you put him through, to allow you to stay here for three months. He's a good man."

"I know but he didn't do it for me. It's because of Genevieve. For the rest of my life, I'll regret hurting Genesis. But you're right, it's time for me to let go and move on."

Chapter Twenty-Three

War Ready

"Look at them bad ass bitches that just pulled up in the drop top beamer," Travis said to Mack as they stood outside in the parking lot of a popular nightclub. It was the thing to do every Thursday night and Mack was there with his crew front and center.

"You right. I ain't neva seen them around here neither. Some new blood," Mack chuckled. "We can be the first to break them in," he smirked.

"I want the one in the passenger seat. You know how much I love a pretty chocolate girl." Travis was already watering at the mouth, imagining how good she would look bent over with her ass up.

"Cool. I'll take the driver or the chick in the backseat." Mack decided.

"I'll take whoever left over," one of the other dudes spoke up and said.

"They look like they waiting on us." Mack licked his lips wishing he could fuck all three of them at the same damn time. The ladies looked like an early Christmas present sitting in their shiny ride. The only thing missing was a big bow.

"Ya gon' stand there or come talk to us?" the chocolate beauty on the passenger side said in a seductive voice.

The guys didn't even try to play it cool. They came rushing towards the car full of eye candy like some dogs in heat.

"You ladies ready to go pop some bottles of bubbly or what," Travis offered.

"We have a better idea." The driver said.

"Really, what's that?" Mack asked.

"We have an amazing present for you sexy motherfuckas."

"I love presents," one of the other dudes said.

"Me too." Mack nodded.

"Who wants their present first." The sexy girl in the backset questioned.

"I do." Travis raised his hand.

"So be it. This present is courtesy of Caleb. Lights out niggas!" The women pulled out their heat simultaneously, catching the men off guard. They were all armed but because they were so busy thinking with their dicks, none of them were prepared to reach for their weapons in a time efficient manner.

"Oh shit!" was all you heard the dudes say as the bullets came spraying, taking each of them down. Other patrons in the parking lot began screaming and scattering for cover. But the hit was so sweet and clean, it took the ladies less than two minutes to handle the job and be out without any repercussions.

Caleb watched in amusement as his hired shooters eliminated Mack and his crew with such ease. When their car sped away, leaving the dead bodies of his enemies, Caleb smiled, pleased with the outcome.

"Them chicks bad." Floyd grinned, looking over at Caleb who was sitting in the driver's seat. "Ain't nothin' like some sexy broads who can handle a gun. Them niggas didn't stand a chance."

"Sure didn't. Mack, the one who wanted to go to war. I ended the shit before it could even get started."

"You did right, Caleb. As you like to say... always be proactive. Delondo's dead, we got rid of them niggas, what's next?" Floyd questioned.

"It's time to get rid of the weakest link. Arnez has to go. He no longer serves a purpose," Caleb stated. "Once I get rid of him, Philly is mine."

It was a beautiful Saturday afternoon and everyone besides Genesis and Talisa were in Miami to attend Aaliyah's wedding. Amir was getting ready to take his seat when he noticed an unknown call pop up on his screen. He was going to ignore it but then he realized it could be his father. Since his mother and father left for their around the world vacation, anytime Genesis would call the number came up either private or unknown.

"Hello."

"Good afternoon, Amir!" a jubilant voice said.

"Who is this?"

"I'm having difficulties reaching your father, so I figured you would be able to assist me."

"Who is this?" Amir raised his voice and demanded to know. He was annoyed he had to figure out who the fuck was on his phone.

"Calm down, Amir. It's your Uncle Arnez."

Amir damn near dropped his phone when he heard the name.

"This has to be a joke. Arnez is dead."

"I'm like the devil, I never die," Arnez boasted in the most sickening way.

"Trust me, when my father finds out you're alive, your death will be imminent," Amir stated boldly.

"We can discuss that later. Right now, I need you to get a message to Genesis."

"What message is that?" Amir was biting down on his lip. He was itching to get his hands on Arnez.

"Tell your father I can only babysit his beautiful daughter but for so long. I'm not really the baby type. My lack of patience and horrific temper doesn't allow it," Arnez huffed.

Amir swallowed hard wanting to believe Arnez was bluffing but he highly doubted it. "Are you saying you have Genevieve?"

"Ding, ding, ding...you are correct. As an added bonus, I have Skylar too. But I'm sure now that Genesis has his beloved Talisa back, he could care less about his baby mama. But I can only imagine how much he loves this beautiful baby girl," Arnez enthused.

"You better not hurt Genevieve, Arnez, or I will kill you myself."

"Don't write a check yo' young ass can't cash, Amir. Now listen, I have to go. Your father has forty-eight hours to get in touch with me. If I don't hear from him, I'ma start sending body parts through Fedex, one at a time." Arnez laughed obnoxiously before ending the call.

Amir's anger had him ready to roar at the top of his lungs but Aaliyah's wedding wasn't the place to do so. Instead he placed the hardest phone call he ever had to make.

"Hello."

"Dad, it's me Amir."

"I figured that, what's going on? Aren't you supposed to be at Aaliyah's wedding?"

"I'm here now but it hasn't started yet. I needed to speak with you about something extremely important." Amir sounded shaky.

"Are you having problems with business?"

"No, nothing like that. This is much worse," Amir's voice cracked.

"Son, talk to me. Tell me what's going on. Whatever it is, we'll get through it."

"Arnez is alive," Amir blurted out.

"What! Are you sure?!"

"Positive. I just got off the phone with him."

"That sonofabitch! That nigga refuses to die."

"It gets worse."

"How can anything be worse than Arnez still being alive?"

"He has Skylar and Genevieve."

"That sick motherfucker. I guess he doesn't know Genevieve isn't my daughter. Listen, I feel horrible for that little girl. If I could, I would save her. But Skylar and Genevieve are no longer my responsibility. I can't allow Arnez to pull me in. He tried to take someone who he figured was the most precious thing to me and it backfired. Arnez will be dealt with but after your mother and I get back from our trip. Make sure you let everyone know to be on alert and we'll deal with it once I'm home. You call me if you need me, son."

"Dad, wait!" Amir yelled out before his father could hang up.

"What is it? Your mother is waiting for me. We're about to go out for dinner," Genesis told him.

"Please don't hate me."

"Amir, you're my son. I could never hate you."

"Genevieve is your daughter!" Amir blurted out.

"Excuse me?"

"Mom was in so much pain. You couldn't see it but the baby was taking you away from us and pulling you closer to Skylar. I just wanted you and mom to be happy again."

"Amir, what have you done."

"When mom told me where you were having the paternity test done, I paid off the guy."

"Did he even do the test?"

"Yes. When it came back you were the father, I had him change the results. I never imagined Genevieve would be in danger."

"You saw the pain I was in when I was told Genevieve wasn't mine. I had to leave New York because I couldn't bear being in the same city as her. You were gonna keep me away from my own flesh and blood...your sister."

"Dad, I'm so, so sorry."

"Sorry isn't enough," Genesis avowed. "We're heading home tonight. You better pray nothing happens to my daughter. I will deal with you when I get back. In the meantime, get our men together. Let them know we're taking Arnez down once and for all so everyone, including you, needs to be war ready."

Coming Soon

A KING PRODUCTION

The Legacy

Keep The Family Close...

A Novel

JOY DEJA KING

Raised By Wolves

Chapter One

"Alejo, we've been doing business for many years and my intention is for there to be many more. But I do have some concerns..."

"That's why we're meeting today," Alejo interjected, cutting Allen off. I've made you a very wealthy man. You've made millions and millions of dollars from my family..."

"And you've made that and much more from our family," Clayton snapped, this time being the one to cut Alejo off. "So, let's acknowledge this being a mutual beneficial relationship between both of our families."

Alejo slit his eyes at Clayton, feeling disrespected his anger rested upon him. Clayton was the youngest son of Allen Collins but also the most vocal. Alejo then turned towards his eldest son Damacio who sat calmly not saying a word in his father's defense, which further enraged the dictator of the Hernandez family.

An ominous quietness engulfed the room as the Collins family remained seated on one side of the table and the Hernandez family occupied the other.

"I think we can agree that over the years we've created a successful business relationship that works for all parties involved," Kasir spoke up and said, trying to be the voice of reason and peacemaker for what was quickly turning into enemy territory. "No one wants to create new problems. We only want to fix the one we currently have so we can all move forward."

"Kasir, I've always liked you," Alejo said with a half smile. "You've continuously conducted yourself with class and respect. Others can learn a lot from you."

"Others, meaning your crooked ass nephews," Clayton barked not ignoring the jab Alejo was taking at him. He then pointed his finger at Felipe and Hector, making sure that everyone at the table knew exactly who he was speaking of since there were a dozen family members on the Hernandez side of the table.

Chaos quickly erupted within the Hernandez family as the members began having a heated exchange amongst each other. They were speaking Spanish and although Allen nor Clayton understood what was being said, Kasir spoke the language fluently.

"Dad, I think we need to fall back and not let this meeting get any further out of control. Let's table this discussion for a later date," Kasir told his father in a very low tone.

"Fuck that! We ain't tabling shit. As much money as we bring to this fuckin' table and these snakes want to short us. Nah, I ain't having it. That shit ends today," Clayton stated, not backing down.

"You come here and insult me and my family with your outrageous accusations," Alejo stood up and yelled, pushing back the single silver curl that kept falling over his forehead. I will not tolerate such insults from the likes of you. My family does good business. You clearly cannot say the same."

"This is what you call good business," Clayton shot back, placing his iPhone on the center of the table. Then pressing play on the video that was sent to him.

Alejo grabbed the phone from off the table and watched the video intently, scrutinizing every detail. After he was satisfied he then handed it to his son Damacio, who after viewing, passed it around to the other family members at the table.

"What's on that video?" Kasir questioned his brother.

"I want to know the same thing," his father stated.

"Let's just say that not only is those two motherfuckers stealing from us, they stealing from they own fuckin' family too," Clayton huffed, leaning back in his chair, pleased that he had the proof to back up his claims.

"We owe your family an apology," Damacio said, as his father sat back down in his chair with a glaze of defeat in his eyes. It was obvious the old man hated to be wrong and had no intentions of admitting it, so his son had to do it for him.

"Does that mean my concerns will be addressed and handled properly?" Allen Collins questioned.

"Of course. You have my word that this matter will be corrected in the very near future and there is no need for you to worry, as it won't happen again. Please accept my apology on behalf of my entire family," Damacio said, reaching over to shake each of their hands.

"Thank you, Damacio," Allen said giving a firm handshake. "I'll be in touch soon."

"Of course. Business will resume as usual and we look forward to it," Damacio made clear before the men gathered their belongings and began to make their exit.

"Wait!" the Collins men stopped in their tracks and turned towards Alejo who had shouted for them to wait.

"Father, what are you doing?" Damacio asked, confused by his sudden outburst.

"There is something that needs to be addressed and no one is leaving this room until it's done," Alejo demanded.

With smooth ease, Clayton rested his arm towards the back of his pants, placing his hand on the Glock 20-10mm auto. Before the meeting, the Collins' men had agreed to have their security team wait outside in the parking lot instead of coming in the building, so it wouldn't be a hostile environment. But that didn't stop Clayton from taking his own precautions. He eyed his brother Kasir who maintained his typical calm demeanor that annoyed the fuck out of Clayton.

"Alejo, what else needs to be said that wasn't already discussed?" Allen asked, showing no signs of distress.

"Please, come take a seat," Alejo said politely. Allen stared at Alejo then turned to his two sons and nodded his head as the three men walked back towards their chairs.

Alejo wasted no time and immediately began his over the top speech. "I was born in Mexico and raised by wolves. I was taught that you kill or be killed. When I rose to power by slaughtering my enemies and my friends, I felt no shame." Alejo stated looking around at everyone sitting at the table. His son Damacio swallowed hard as his adam's apple seemed to be throbbing out of his neck.

"As I got older and had my own family, I decided I didn't want that for my children. I wanted them to understand the importance of loyalty, honor and respect," Alejo said proudly, speaking with his thick Spanish accent, which was heavier than usual. He moved away from his chair and began to pace the floor as his spoke. "Without understanding the meaning of being loyal, honoring and respecting your family, you're worthless. Family forgives but some things are unforgivable so you have no place on this earth or in my family."

Then without warning and before anyone had even noticed, all you saw was blood squirting from Felipe's slit throat. Then with the same precision and quickness, Alejo took his sharp pocketknife and slit Hector's throat too. Everyone was too stunned and taken aback to stutter a word.

Alejo wiped the blood off his pocketknife on the white shirt that a now dead Felipe was wearing. He kept wiping until the knife was clean. "That is what happens when you are disloyal. It will not be tolerated...ever." Alejo made direct contact with each of his family members at the round table before focusing on Allen. "I want to personally apologize to you and your sons. I do not condone what Felipe and Hector did and they have now paid the price with their lives."

"Apology accepted," Allen said.

"Yeah, now let's get the fuck outta here," Clayton whispered to his father as the three men stood in unison not speaking another word until they were out the building.

"What type of shit was that?" Kasir mumbled.

"I told you that old man was fuckin' crazy," Clayton said shaking his head as they got into their waiting SUV.

"I think we all knew he was crazy just not that crazy. Alejo know he could've slit them boys' throats after we left," Allen huffed. "He just wanted us to see the fuckin' blood too and ruin our afternoon," he added before chuckling.

"I think it was more than just that," Clayton replied, looking out the tinted window as the driver pulled out the parking lot.

"Then what?" Kasir questioned.

"I think old man Alejo was trying to make a point, not only to his family members but to us too."

"You might be right, Clayton."

"I know I'm right. We need to keep all eyes on Alejo 'cause I don't trust him. He might've killed his crooked ass nephews to show good faith but trust me that man hates to ever be wrong about anything. What he did to his nephews is probably what he really wanted to do to us but he knew nobody would've left that building alive. The only truth Alejo spoke in there was he was raised by wolves," Clayton scoffed leaning back in the car seat.

All three men remained silent for the duration of the drive. Each pondering what had transpired in what was supposed to be a simple business meeting that turned into a double homicide. They also thought about the point Clayton said Alejo was trying to make. No one wanted that to be true as their business with the Hernandez family was a lucrative one for everyone involved. But for men like Alejo, sometimes pride held more value than the almighty dollar, which made him extremely dangerous.

Baller Bitches
THE REUNION
VOLUME 4

JOY DEJA KING

Chapter One

Nothing Seems To Be The Same

The gray skies filled with heavy clouds on the cold winter day satirized the grief looming in the air. The low rumble of distant thunder could be heard as guests arrived for the outdoor graveside funeral service.

"Do you think Blair and Kennedy are coming?" Diamond asked Cameron as they took their seats.

"Honestly..."

"Look," Diamond cut her husband off as she nodded her head towards the arriving cars. "It's

Kennedy. She came," Diamond said smiling. *Please God, let Blair show up too,* she prayed to herself.

As if the angels heard her pleas, a few minutes later a chauffeur-driven, black tinted Rolls Royce Phantom pulled up.

"Mommy, mommy, Auntie Blair is here!" Elijah exclaimed when she stepped out the car. "Do you think Donovan came?"

"I don't think so, sweetie." Diamond smiled, patting her son's head.

"I still can't believe she went back to that dude," Cameron shook his head and said as Blair and Skee Patron arrived hand in hand.

"All that matters is that she showed up... both of them," Diamond said, thrilled to see her best friends.

It had been a year since Diamond had spoken to Blair or Kennedy. Never did she imagine their reunion would take place at a funeral. Life had torn them apart, it seemed it took death to bring them back together.

A King Production

ORDER FORM

Name:

Address:

City/State:

Zip:

QUANTITY	TITLES	PRICE	TOTAL
	Bitch	$15.00	
	Bitch Reloaded	$15.00	
	The Bitch Is Back	$15.00	
	Queen Bitch	$15.00	
	Last Bitch Standing	$15.00	
	Superstar	$15.00	
	Ride Wit' Me	$12.00	
	Ride Wit' Me Part 2	$15.00	
	Stackin' Paper	$15.00	
	Trife Life To Lavish	$15.00	
	Trife Life To Lavish II	$15.00	
	Stackin' Paper II	$15.00	
	Rich or Famous	$15.00	
	Rich or Famous Part 2	$15.00	
	Rich or Famous Part 3	$15.00	
	Bitch A New Beginning	$15.00	
	Mafia Princess Part 1	$15.00	
	Mafia Princess Part 2	$15.00	
	Mafia Princess Part 3	$15.00	
	Mafia Princess Part 4	$15.00	
	Mafia Princess Part 5	$15.00	
	Boss Bitch	$15.00	
	Baller Bitches Vol. 1	$15.00	
	Baller Bitches Vol. 2	$15.00	
	Baller Bitches Vol. 3	$15.00	
	Bad Bitch	$15.00	
	Still The Baddest Bitch	$15.00	
	Power	$15.00	
	Power Part 2	$15.00	
	Drake	$15.00	
	Drake Part 2	$15.00	
	Female Hustler	$15.00	
	Female Hustler Part 2	$15.00	
	Female Hustler Part 3	$15.00	
	Female Hustler Part 4	$15.00	
	Princess Fever "Birthday Bash"	$9.99	
	Nico Carter The Men Of The Bitch Series	$15.00	
	Bitch The Beginning Of The End	$15.00	
	Supreme...Men Of The Bitch Series	$15.00	
	Bitch The Final Chapter	$15.00	
	Stackin' Paper III	$15.00	
	Men Of The Bitch Series And The Women Who Love Them	$15.00	
	Coke Like The 80s	$15.00	
	Baller Bitches The Reunion Vol. 4	$15.00	
	Stackin' Paper IV	$15.00	
	The Legacy	$15.00	

Shipping/Handling (Via Priority Mail) $6.75 1-2 Books, $8.95 3-4 Books add $1.95 for ea. Additional book.

Total: $_____ **FORMS OF ACCEPTED PAYMENTS:** Certified or government issued checks and money Orders, all ma

in orders take 5-7 Business days to be delivered